"I'll Never Forgive You for This, Travis. Never!"

She paused. "How could I have been such a fool? I was so careful to be honest with you, telling you everything. I didn't want to keep anything from you, and all the time—"

"Susan, listen to me. I know I should have told you. I would have—"

"When?" Her voice rose shrilly. "I'm leaving you, Travis. You'll hear from my lawyer about the divorce."

JEANNE STEPHENS
loves to travel, but she's always glad to get home to her Oklahoma cattle ranch. This mother of three loves reading ("I'll read anything!" she says), needlework, photography and long walks, during which she works out her latest book.

D1003024

Dear Reader:

During the last year, many of you have written to Silhouette telling us what you like best about Silhouette Romances and, more recently, about Silhouette Special Editions. You've also told us what else you'd like to read from Silhouette. With your comments and suggestions in mind, we've developed SILHOUETTE DESIRE.

SILHOUETTE DESIREs will be on sale this June, and each month we'll bring you four new DESIREs written by some of your favorite authors—Stephanie James, Diana Palmer, Rita Clay, Suzanne Simms and many more.

SILHOUETTE DESIREs may not be for everyone, but they are for those readers who want a more sensual, provocative romance. The heroines are slightly older—women who are actively involved in their careers and the world around them. If you want to experience all the excitement, passion and joy of falling in love, then SILHOUETTE DESIRE is for you.

I'd appreciate any thoughts you'd like to share with us on new SILHOUETTE DESIRE, and I invite you to write to us at the address below:

Karen Solem
Editor-in-Chief
Silhouette Books
P.O. Box 769
New York, N.Y. 10019

JEANNE STEPHENS
Bride in Barbados

Silhouette Special Edition

Published by Silhouette Books New York

America's Publisher of Contemporary Romance

Other Silhouette Books by Jeanne Stephens

Mexican Nights
Wonder and Wild Desire

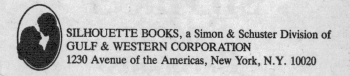

SILHOUETTE BOOKS, a Simon & Schuster Division of
GULF & WESTERN CORPORATION
1230 Avenue of the Americas, New York, N.Y. 10020

Copyright © 1982 by Jeanne Stephens

Distributed by Pocket Books

ISBN: 0-671-53530-7

First Silhouette Books printing June, 1982

10 9 8 7 6 5 4 3 2 1

Map by Tony Ferrara

Bride in
Barbados

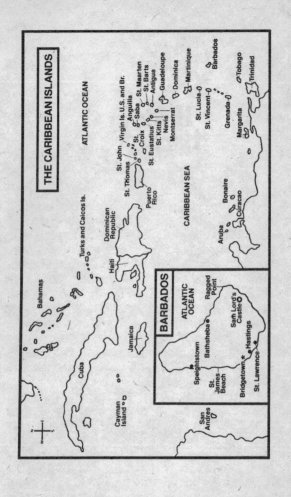

Chapter One

$\mathcal{T}$he dusty Jeep jolted to a stop on the grassy verge at the edge of a field of sugarcane. The green-leafed stalks, taller than a man, spread out across the lowland plateau, following the shape of the coast as far as the eye could see. The sea was calm and quiet, that deep Caribbean blue that has to be seen to be believed. The sky was almost as resplendently colored as the sea, with a few puffy cotton clouds drifting near the horizon. In contrast to the blue of sea and sky, the sand on the narrow beach was white with a trace of pale gold, testimony to its coral reef origin, and the cane was at the height of its lush green and yellow hues.

The door of the Jeep creaked faintly, perhaps protesting at the way it was forcefully thrust back as the driver climbed out. He was a tall man with a hard, lean build, burned bronze by the sun. His hair was black and thick, his brows heavy over brown eyes that caught the hint of color from the sand and reflected it in golden glints. It was clear that a narrowing of the lids, bringing the thick black lashes close together to soften the sun's glare, was habitual, for fans of fine lines were etched deeply at the corners of his eyes.

His wide mouth twisted into an expression that was more a grimace than a smile, the straight line of his teeth flashing white in the surrounding deep tan of his skin. His faded jeans rode low on his hips and, below the knees, were tucked into tall leather boots that were dusty from traversing cane fields and dirt lanes too narrow for a vehicle. His shirt was of blue-gray chambray, spread open almost to his navel to reveal more bronzed skin and black hair glistening with the sweat that had drenched the shirt, pasting it to his solidly muscled midsection and back.

A stained, Western-style straw hat was pushed back from his face, leaving a wide, banded impression across his forehead as evidence of its usual position. The hard angles of his features suggested strength, and a potential for implacability. He had the appearance of a man who did what had to be done unhesitatingly, whatever the consequences.

He gazed, squint-eyed, down the narrow space between the two rows of sugarcane directly in front of him, then with a loose, swinging gait walked into the opening. Pulling a pocket knife from his jeans, Travis Sennett cut a short piece of cane from the nearest plant and examined the cross section with experienced eyes. The stalk was a healthy yellow and oozing juice, progressing toward the perfect maturity made possible by the limey richness of the coral soil and the temperate Barbadian climate.

He tossed the sample aside and pocketed the knife, his eyes moving on down the straight green wall of cane. Its robust perfection seemed to mock him. "Damn you, Harris Sennett!" he muttered softly. Had the old coot really meant to dangle all this beneath his nose for two years, then yank it away? Maybe his grandfather had merely wanted to continue pulling the strings, even from his grave. "To think I got all choked up at your funeral, you capricious old goat! I'll bet you got a laugh out of that, didn't you?"

Hanging his thumbs on the edges of his pants pockets, he moved farther into the cane, stopping now and then to check another stalk. It would be an abundant harvest, possibly the last harvest he would see on the Sennett Plantation. The thought pushed another soft curse from him. . . .

As his hands checked the cane, his mind wandered back to his boyhood when he had come with his parents, at his grandfather's summons, to live on the plantation.

At seven he had been far too young to realize that his father, Lyle, had returned to Barbados because he was too indolent to make something of himself on his own, and too weak to stand up to his father. These character deficiencies ensured that Lyle would dislike almost everything about the plantation. There was plenty of hard physical labor, even for the owner's son, for Harris Sennett believed in working alongside his overseer and field hands often enough to earn their respect.

Lyle had preferred supervising from afar,

preferably a shaded veranda with a frosty piña colada in one hand. Breaking into a sweat while getting his hands dirty alongside the workers was offensive to tastes honed to a discerning sensitivity at exclusive British boarding schools.

When Lyle had ventured to suggest that his rowdy young son could benefit from being shipped off to Lyle's old school, Harris had retorted flatly, "I don't mean to make the same mistake with my grandson that I made with you. Until he's ready for college, Travis can go to school right here on the island."

"You mean a tutor?"

"No tutor!" Harris spat out the word as if its taste disgusted him.

Aghast, Lyle had exclaimed, "Surely you wouldn't send him to that school in town along with slaves' descendants and every ragtag ruffian in the vicinity!"

Harris had snorted, his tone adamant. "I mean to do just that. Travis can take care of himself. He'll grow up with a good, stiff backbone." He did not add, "unlike his father," but the criticism was there in the air between them. Even the seven-year-old Travis had sensed it.

But if Lyle had disliked the plantation, Travis's mother, Mary, had hated it with a passion that far outstripped any emotion elicited by her husband or son. Sometimes in the night, a seven-, eight-, or nine-year-old Travis had been awakened by his mother's shrill berating of his father in their bedroom at the opposite end of a long corridor.

"I'm going crazy, I tell you! I hate this place— this house, this plantation, this hot little pile of coral they call an island! I can't stand it here any longer!"

Once Travis had heard his father say, "When he's gone, we'll sell everything and move back to England. He can't live forever."

His mother's reply had revealed the agony of her frustration. "What makes you think he can't?" And then she had begun to sob and it had taken his father a long time to quiet her.

As it had turned out, Mary had not been overstating her aversion to Barbados. When Travis was ten, she had packed a bag in a fit of hysteria and walked out. The next day Harris learned that his daughter-in-law was staying temporarily on a nearby island, waiting for Lyle to bring her enough money to return to England. Harris sent Lyle after her, not with the demanded money, but to bring her back to the plantation where, according to Harris, she belonged.

In one of those cruel strokes that fate sometimes visits upon men, a long-dormant volcano on the island where Mary had taken refuge erupted. Mary and Lyle Sennett were among the forty people killed, and among the handful whose bodies were never recovered.

Left alone with a stubborn, independent old man whose regard did not manifest itself in demonstrations of affection, even to a ten-year-old grandson, Travis learned stoicism at an early age. More pertinently, he learned self-sufficiency, a self-sufficiency modeled on the curt homespun adages of Harris Sennett: *A man never backs down. A man never runs from a fight. It's no disgrace to get knocked down, but it's the worst sort of disgrace not to get back up swinging. A man has to be more determined and more ruthless than his enemies or he'll take a beating.*

Gradually, as he passed through his teens, Travis became conscious of the void in his life. He missed an occasional gentle motherly caress or a kind fatherly word. He began to blame his grandfather and the plantation for his parents' deaths. He managed, in those crucial adolescent years, to forget Lyle's and Mary's weaknesses, and turned them, in his mind, into martyrs the equal of Joan of Arc and Thomas More. He vowed that, when he graduated from college, he would never again return to Barbados and his grandfather.

Instead, he had gone as a construction engineer to supervise the building of dams, bridges and roads in remote places where the work was the most grueling, the conditions the most primitive, the hours the longest and the pay the highest. The jungles and wildernesses of Guatemala, Brazil, China—for ten years he had traveled from one such out-of-the-way corner of the world to another. Harris's letters occasionally caught up with him, letters threatening everything short of murder if Travis didn't return to Barbados. But Harris no longer had the wherewithal to back up his threats. Travis didn't care who inherited the old man's money; he was his own man at last, and as determined and unbending as his grandfather. The streak of iron that had somehow skipped the son's generation had come out strong and true in the grandson.

Then, two years ago, the old man had tracked him down in Kenya and, over a crackling telephone line, informed Travis that he'd suffered a severe heart attack, that he would be a semi-invalid from then on out, that he needed Travis to take over the plantation and his controlling interest in a Bridgetown bank. There was no one else he could trust.

What demands and threats had failed to do, a weak-voiced plea had accomplished. Travis had gone home.

When he had walked into his grandfather's bedroom, the old man, in cotton pajamas several sizes too large for his shrunken frame, had been sitting propped up in bed with business papers and account books scattered across the rumpled sheets. Travis had been stunned at how frail and old he looked.

Slowly, Harris's still sharp hazel eyes had traveled up the long length of his grandson before he observed, "Well, I hope you're through punishing me for my myriad sins. We've a hell-uva lot of work to do."

In the two years that had followed, Travis had gained a grudging respect for his grandfather. Running a vast sugar plantation while supervising the affairs of a good-sized bank on the side was a herculean task. But it wasn't long before he knew that this green and verdant land was where he belonged.

Never one to praise overmuch, Harris had nonetheless made it clear that he was well satisfied with his grandson's management of his affairs. "It'll all be yours when I'm gone, Travis," he had said. "You've proved you're man enough to handle it." There had been frequent speeches, too, about the importance of keeping everything in the family, the implications of which Travis had not seen at the time. "It's time you married and had a family," Harris had told him on several occasions, "a son who can take over here when he's needed. You shouldn't have to stay in the driver's seat as long as I have."

It wasn't that Travis meant never to marry, but a wedding wasn't in his plans for the foreseeable future. Once, Kay Harte, a friend since childhood, had accused him of never having been in love. Until then Travis hadn't given it much thought, but he guessed Kay was right. He'd lost count of the number of women he had known, but none of them had ever made him want to hang around long after he had, to use the old-fashioned phrase, had his way with her. He'd assumed he still had plenty of time before he must think about giving up his freedom. His grandfather had had other ideas. . . .

Abruptly, Travis reversed his direction and returned to the Jeep. Anger made him grind the gears before, grim-faced, he drove toward the plantation great house.

As always, the sight of the stately old mansion sent a feeling compounded of pride and family continuity through him. Built in 1690 of coral stone by the son of one of Barbados's first British colonists, it had been in the Sennett family ever since. Its wide, white two-story expanse, red-roofed with dozens of green-awninged windows, sat in an oasis of encircling trees and neatly landscaped gardens and lawn. Travis turned the Jeep into a palm-fringed avenue that led to a cluster of white frame structures of much more recent origin—gardeners' sheds, workshops, garages—at the back of the house. He left the Jeep in one of ten garage stalls and walked toward the kitchen entrance.

Mala Jaimes, a descendant of the slaves brought to the Sennett Plantation in the 1700s, who, along with her married daughter, Amii, ran the house, glanced up curiously as Travis stalked through the kitchen on his way to the study.

Upon entering the maple-paneled, leather-furnished room where he conducted most of his business, Travis tossed his hat on a chair and, going to the bar concealed in a section of the bookshelves, poured himself a shot of rum.

He drank, then his eyes traveled to the desk and he walked across the room. He set his drink down and picked up the folded sheet of white paper that was anchored by a pink conch shell.

His grandfather's will was short and to the point. Reading the words again, Travis discovered that his feeling of betrayal was almost as strong now as it had been the first time three days ago, the day after Harris's funeral, when he had discovered the will in the study wall safe.

A hefty portfolio of stocks and bonds was left to Curt Winston and Violet Winston Graves, the children of Harris's daughter in England. The remainder of the estate—the plantation and bank in Bridgetown—were left wholly to Travis, upon one condition: that he produce a legitimate heir by the time he was thirty-five. If he did not, the entire estate was to be split three ways, an equal share going to each of Harris's three grandchildren.

Harris had given Travis fifteen months in

which to marry and father a child, or he could say goodbye to all that he had come to cherish so deeply. Travis had no doubt whatever that, should everything be apportioned equally, the Barbadian interests would be sold, for neither Curt nor Violet had the slightest interest in them. They did, however, have a burning desire to live in a much more luxurious style in England than the one to which they were accustomed.

Travis downed the rest of the rum and, clutching the will, left the study with purposeful strides. At the foot of the stairs, he shouted, "Mala!"

The small round-faced woman appeared promptly, as if she had been expecting the summons. "What you want, Mistah Travis?" Her voice was rich with the melodious Bajun patois.

"Call the airlines and get me on the next flight to Miami."

Mala regarded him with the same disapproving stare she had used on him as a child. "Why I not know you goin' on dis trip? I fixin' you a feast for dinner, mon."

"I just decided to go," replied Travis, his words short with impatience to follow through on his sudden decision. "I'm sorry about dinner, Mala. Why don't you feed it to Abraham and Jim?" He named her husband and son-in-law, both of whom worked for him. "I'm going up to shower and pack a few things. Let me know how soon I can leave. Oh, and after you get the flight reservation, you might phone Tony Valdez and tell him I'll be coming to his office from the airport—unless it's after five, in which case I'll go directly to his house."

"Valdez? You mean Mistah Harris's lawyer?"

"That's right."

"When you comin' back?"

"Two or three days. I'm not sure. Just leave the return open."

Mala heaved a put-upon sigh. "Rush, rush— all dis rush. Oh, mon, you always was a heap o' tribulation."

Travis grinned and, without waiting for further objections from Mala, bounded up the carpeted stairs two at a time. The old man might have thought he'd had the last laugh, but now that Travis had his wind back, he wasn't taking this lying down. "Harris," he muttered as he crossed the threshold of his bedroom, "thanks for the advice. I'm on my feet now—and swinging."

The traffic was enough to make even that jungle in Kenya he'd left two years ago seem attractive, Travis thought as he deftly sidestepped a taxi and gained the curb. The taxi's horn blared and Travis turned to wave at the fuming Puerto Rican driver.

The driver thrust his head out the window. *"Pare!* You wish to die?" He shook a fist at Travis. *"Loco hombre!"*

"Likewise!" Travis called back before turning to scan the facades of the office buildings on the block. The Blaylock Building was only two doors east of where he stood. He had walked from the downtown hotel he'd checked into at two that morning, after deciding it would be the better part of wisdom not to get Valdez out of bed at that hour of the night. No point in riling the man whose help he was going to need before he'd even had a chance to tell Valdez why he was there.

He'd reached Valdez's secretary at nine and been given a ten o'clock appointment. She'd rearranged some other appointments to work him in after receiving Mala's phone call the day before. She made it clear that she wouldn't do that for any Tom, Dick or Harry who walked in off the street. But since he had come so far and his business was apparently urgent . . .

Stifling his impatience, Travis had managed to sound properly grateful. Entering the air-conditioned building, Travis shrugged his shoulders to settle the warm weight of his pearl gray jacket more comfortably on his shoulders. He stood beside the bank of closed elevator doors and ran a finger around the perspiring skin of his neck inside the stiff white collar. It was even warmer in downtown Miami than at home. Whatever breezes might have been wafting in from the ocean were cut off by the tall buildings.

In the crush of bodies riding up in the elevator, Travis glanced down at the cute redhead, in a too tight clinging jersey dress, beside him and caught her giving him the once over. The challenge in her smile made his lips twitch and he lowered one eyelid in the suggestion of a wink. A shame he didn't have the time to make the young lady's acquaintance. Unfortunately, more important matters demanded his attention.

Valdez's starched, middle-aged secretary looked as aloof and proper as her voice had sounded on the telephone.

"You're fifteen minutes early, Mr. Sennett. Mr. Valdez still has another client in his office." Although a head shorter than he, she somehow managed to look down her nose at him.

"I don't mind waiting." Travis sat in a chair of white molded plastic that felt as if it had been designed for some being other than man. Shifting uncomfortably, he took in the white shag carpeting with its large black geometric design, the plastic cubes of yellow and black that served as tables, the chairs identical to the one in which he sat, and decided he was right. Surely this was a set from a science fiction movie.

"Mr. Valdez wanted to know the nature of your business, but I was unable to enlighten him." The secretary watched him squirm in the chair with a superior expression on her pinched face. "The woman who called yesterday had a most—ah, peculiar accent. I hardly understood half of what she said. If you will tell me a little more than you did on the phone earlier, I can pull the proper files."

"That won't be necessary. I have all we'll need right here." Travis patted the jacket pocket that held Harris Sennett's will.

Her eyes made a quick appraising survey of him, a tiny nerve near the corner of her thin mouth jerking as if she were marshalling her small reserves of patience. Then the telephone on her desk rang, distracting her. While she was still speaking into the receiver, Valdez's office door opened and an elderly woman came out, followed by the short, fleshy olive-skinned lawyer himself.

"Now don't you worry about a thing, Mrs. Harelson. All is in good order and we should get a hearing with the probate judge within the next few days."

The woman smiled uncertainly before she crossed the reception area and left the suite.

"Travis! How in the world are you?" Valdez's smooth pudgy fingers gripped Travis's calloused hand.

"I've been better," Travis observed dryly. "That's what I want to talk to you about."

Hesitation glimmered in the other man's dark eyes, but it was quickly banished as Valdez said jovially, "Come on in, man."

Travis followed him into a generous-sized office soothingly decorated in subdued earth tones. The Florida sun was filtering through the loosely woven beige draperies that covered the large window behind the massive golden oak desk. Travis sank gratefully into a well-stuffed leather armchair. "I see the decorator didn't get past your office door, thank God."

Valdez looked puzzled for a moment, then made a dismissive gesture with one arm. "Oh, you mean the reception area? My wife is responsible for that, I'm afraid. I convinced her that my office must remain inviolate." He sat behind the desk and leaned back in his chair. "Now, what can I do for you?"

Travis pulled the will from his pocket and tossed it on the desk. Valdez picked it up, scanned it briefly then handed it back. "I know what it says. Your grandfather mailed me a copy. He wanted me to know that the earlier will my former partner had drawn up for him had been superceded."

Travis raised a questioning eyebrow. "What was in the earlier one?"

Valdez studied him for a moment. "It divided everything between his daughter in England and your father. He made it about a year before your parents died. I reminded him several times during the past ten years—ever since Mr. Brandt retired and I took over his clients—that he ought to make a new will. He always said he would when he was ready."

A trace of a smile twisted Travis's mouth. "He almost waited too long." The new will was dated less than a month before Harris Sennett's death.

"Evidently he knew he hadn't much longer to live."

"Yeah," Travis agreed sardonically. "I watched him fight it for two years, but even Harris Sennett had to admit defeat eventually. Except he didn't quite, did he?"

Valdez sat forward in his chair and waited. "Tell me, Tony," Travis went on, "are you interested in handling my legal affairs now that my grandfather is gone?"

The lawyer's expression was eager, yet guarded. "Certainly I am, Travis. I'm already familiar with your grandfather's business, so I can do a better job for you than anyone else. If you would like, I can supply several references. I think you'll find my professional reputation is above reproach."

"I won't need references, Tony. I had you

thoroughly checked out soon after I returned to Barbados and took over the management of my grandfather's affairs."

Surprise flashed across Valdez's face to be followed by a grudging respect. "Are you saying you've already decided to retain me as your attorney?"

Travis regarded him with assessing eyes before he nodded. "The first thing I want you to do is to break that will."

"On what grounds?"

Travis's narrowed gaze was hard. "The old man was dying. He couldn't have been in total command of his mental faculties." The desperation of his own personal situation brought an edge of ruthlessness to his voice.

The attorney took a long breath and gazed at a plaque in a corner of the room for a moment. Then his eyes came back to Travis's rugged face. "It won't work, Travis. Your grandfather consulted an attorney on Barbados about the wording. There aren't any loopholes. He also took the precaution of flying in a psychiatrist from the Mayo Clinic. The doctor gave him a thorough examination and wrote a detailed report of Mr. Sennett's mental and emotional condition at the time the will was made. I believe your grandfather said he'd deposited a copy of the report with that Barbadian attorney—Wrigley or Wiggins, something like that. Didn't you know about it?"

A sinking sensation pressed into the pit of Travis's stomach. "Wiggins," he murmured. He knew the man. He was young, but a good lawyer. Not in Valdez's league, maybe, but he had apparently seen that Harris covered all the bases.

"And, no, I didn't know about Wiggins or the psychiatrist. Evidently this all transpired during the two days I was in New York on bank business. No wonder the old man was so anxious for me to go."

Valdez smiled. "You have to admit he handled everything shrewdly. Doesn't sound like an unstable man to me."

"Dammit, Tony!" Travis came to his feet in indignation. "He promised me that the Barbadian holdings would be mine. My blood and guts are in that plantation now. For two years he told me I'd earned the right to take over there, and I have!"

"You are free, of course, to consult another attorney—or several others. But if you want my opinion, Travis, you'll only be wasting a lot of time and money if you pursue this."

Travis moved restlessly about the room, then returned to his chair and folded his long frame into it. "No. I trust you. I'll take your word for it, but I don't like it. If I'd known what Harris was up to, all the whining and pleading in the world wouldn't have brought me back to Barbados."

Elbows planted on his desk, Valdez brought the tips of his pudgy fingers together. "Can you scrape together enough in the next fifteen months to buy out your cousins' interests?"

Travis's look was pungent. "Are you aware of how much property on the island is worth these days?" He shook his head. "Not a chance. Not without selling some land, which I won't do."

"And you're not willing to give it all up?"

"No," Travis countered emphatically.

"That leaves you with only one recourse. Get

yourself a wife and get her pregnant as quickly as you can." Travis's look was scornful. Unaffected, Valdez continued, "Untold numbers of men have found themselves faced with less attractive alternatives." He grinned drolly. "Surely there must be one or two ladies tucked away somewhere who wouldn't mind becoming Mrs. Travis Sennett."

"Under the circumstances," Travis retorted sarcastically, "I wouldn't count on it."

"Come on Travis." The lawyer's tone attempted to coax Travis into a better frame of mind. "Marriages are made every day for less noble reasons than to perpetuate a family dynasty."

Although it didn't make his situation any more tolerable, Travis knew the man was right. In his initial shock and anger he had so far forgotten himself as to confide in Kay Harte the conditions of his grandfather's will. She had made it clear that she'd be willing to marry him. He had suspected for a long time that Kay was in love with him, but he didn't feel the same way about her. He had always taken her for granted, and he knew that he would continue to do so. He'd make Kay a rotten husband and, besides, the thought of spending the rest of his life with her gave him a claustrophobic feeling. No, that alternative was definitely out. Because he knew she genuinely wanted the best for him, though, he had phoned Kay before his departure to let her know what course of action he had decided to take.

"Do my cousins know the terms of the will yet?"

"Mr. Winston called me yesterday," Valdez

admitted. "I had to put him in the picture. He's one of the heirs, after all."

"Curt and Violet couldn't be bothered with coming to the funeral," Travis muttered resentfully, "but you can bet they'll be on my doorstep on my thirty-fifth birthday."

"They'd have no reason to be if you're married and a father by then."

Valdez's calm assumption that his position wasn't as unacceptable as Travis seemed to think irritated Travis. "You're a big help!"

"I've given you my best advice. That will is airtight."

"Well . . ." Travis got to his feet. "I'll keep you informed, Tony." He started for the door, then stopped to add with black humor, "I don't suppose you know the name of a good marriage broker. Somebody ought to put out a catalogue for us poor lovelorn creatures who are in the market for spouses."

"Somebody probably has," Valdez observed wryly.

"Probably." Travis lifted his hand in a half-hearted salute and left the office.

He lunched in a Chinese restaurant near the Blaylock Building. Leaving the restaurant afterward, he shucked his jacket and tie, draped them across his shoulder and walked the streets for hours, trying to see some acceptable way out of his dilemma that he and Tony Valdez had missed. It was a futile undertaking. The old man had him in a box.

Finally, he turned his steps toward his hotel, arriving there after six. He was hot, rumpled, tired and, for the moment, defeated. He had wrestled his thoughts around so long that he had a thundering headache. He didn't want to think about his problems anymore. He didn't want to think about anything, at least until he'd had a night's sound sleep.

He was so wrung out that when he reached his room, he fell into a chair, intending to rest briefly before getting cleaned up. Instead, he fell asleep and stayed that way for almost two hours.

He awoke feeling only slightly refreshed, but his headache wasn't pounding as loudly as before. After showering and dressing in tan trousers and a cream linen dinner jacket, he decided that what he needed was the biggest steak the hotel had to offer and several good stiff drinks, after which he would fall into bed and know nothing thereafter until morning.

Chapter Two

A wide silver slave bracelet flashed as Susan Warren ran a brush through the tumbling length of her silver-blond hair. She turned sideways, head slightly tilted, to scrutinize the slender lines of her floor-length gown. The black crepe, stitched all over with threads that glittered under the lights, was fastened on one shoulder, leaving the other shoulder and both arms bare. Split to above the knee on one side, it hugged her figure provocatively. Black spike-heeled spaghetti-strap sandals further enhanced her long, leggy look.

Satisfied, she laid her brush aside and, leaning closer to the mirror, brushed blue-gray eyeshadow on her lids, a color that emphasized the blue highlights in her emerald eyes. She had well-proportioned patrician features and dark brows and lashes that needed little makeup ordinarily, but the glaring lights under which she performed made her ivory complexion, even with the light tan she had acquired since coming to Miami a few months earlier, look washed out without generously applied cosmetics. Her mascara was heavier and her lip gloss darker than she wore when she wasn't singing and, except for evening wear, she hardly ever used eye shadow at all.

The dressing room was too warm. It was situated in a ground floor corner of the hotel far removed from the central air-conditioning unit, and the air flowing from the vents was usually thin and not very cool. Since Susan's personal situation made it unwise to ask favors of the hotel club manager, Dirk Cantino, she had brought a small electric fan from her apartment. It sat on a worn wicker chair and she moved closer to it as her emerald gaze flicked to her wristwatch. It was eight forty-five, still ten minutes too early to go along the corridor to the hotel's expensive supper club, the Top Hat, for the first of her two nightly performances.

She turned to allow the fan to blow on her from another angle and, sighing, wondered how much longer she would be able to keep the job she'd obtained just three months earlier. She had managed to hold Dirk Cantino at arm's length thus far, but it was becoming more difficult. The last thing she wanted was to get involved with someone like Dirk, who was egotistical, shallow and impractical beneath a thick layer of charm.

She had left New Orleans four months ago after breaking her ten-month engagement to Frank Rosler, a man very like Dirk. It had taken her a long time to see through Frank's veneer and realize that he was never going to be any more stable or mature than he already was, that he would spend his life drifting from one get-rich-quick scheme to another, and probably one meaningless affair to another, even if she gave in to his pleas and married him. The charming, considerate man she had thought she loved was merely an attractive shell; the real Frank Rosler was quite a different person.

Consequently she was totally immune to the same surface attractiveness in her new boss. The problem was that Dirk, unaccustomed to being brushed off by women, refused to believe it.

A sharp tap sounded on the dressing room door. "Susan! You decent?" Without giving her time to do anything about it had she not been, Dirk Cantino opened the door and stepped inside. His light blue eyes roamed over her figure appreciatively before coming to rest on her face. "Sweetheart, you look delicious enough to make a man want to take a bite."

"He'd better not, unless he's looking for an acute case of indigestion," Susan retorted. "I once studied judo, remember?"

Irritation hesitated in his expression before he laughed, tossing a wayward lock of blond hair back from his forehead. "You're a great little kidder, honey." He strolled over to her and lifted a curling strand of silver-blond hair between two fingers, an intimate gesture that infuriated Susan. "How would you like to come up to my room after the last show for a nightcap? I've got a big deal in the making, and there could be something in it for you."

"That's nice." She had to resist a desire to slap his hand away from her hair.

"There's a chance I can go to one of the best hotels in Vegas as club manager, with stock in the corporation as a part of my salary. What do you think of that?"

"I hope it works out for you, Dirk." She had heard about too many of his "big deals" to believe it would, but she meant it sincerely. It would be a relief not to have to work for him any longer and be able to keep her job at the same time.

"They need singers in Vegas, honey. It's the big time. And I'll be in a position to help you. Come upstairs later and we'll discuss it."

Unable to submit to his touch any longer, Susan moved her head to one side to release the lock of hair he was holding and stepped back, putting the chair and fan between them. "Thanks, but I can't make it tonight." She looked pointedly at her watch. "I'd better go. I'm on in ten minutes." She switched off the fan.

Dirk followed her from the dressing room. "Think it over, Susan. I'll have drinks and a tray of canapes waiting, and it would be a shame to waste them."

Susan, who had hurried ahead of him down the corridor, pretended not to hear. She turned a corner, taking the hall that led to a side door of the club near the raised platform where she did her act.

Jacky Thornton, a balding man barely five feet tall who acted as MC and played piano for her, greeted her as she stepped into the shadowy corner at the back of the stage.

"Hiya, Susie. You okay tonight? How's the throat?"

"The scratchy feeling's gone, Jacky. Looks as if it wasn't a cold coming on after all, thank heaven. What kind of house do we have to-night?"

"The place is full. They seem like a pretty friendly bunch, too. Hey, I like that dress."

Susan smiled fondly at the little man. "Thank you, Sir. Are you ready?"

Jacky walked to the microphone, a cue to a man at the back of the room to flip the switches controlling the spotlights. There was a low mur-muring, followed by a smattering of applause. Jacky told a few jokes to warm up the crowd before introducing Susan.

She sang a Rogers and Hammerstein medley followed by some more recent folky tunes. She had the sort of low, sultry singing voice that fit slow, often melancholy, songs.

As she sang, she realized that Jacky was right. It was a friendly crowd, and they were respond-ing well to her. She was halfway through her act before she recognized the dark, striking looking man in a light-colored dinner jacket as the same man who had sat through both her performanc-es the night before. As on the previous evening, he sat alone at a table near the stage and watched her with narrowed eyes.

There was a lancing penetration in his look that sent a small, unsettling shiver up her back-bone. She had been in the business long enough not to let the customers distract her, even the occasional drunken heckler who had to be invit-ed to leave by the manager. But if this man had had too much alcohol, he held it extremely well. Maybe it was his deeply thoughtful expression, as if he were trying to pin down where he had known her before, that gave her the slight feeling of discomposure. She knew, however, that his thoughts must be on a very different track, for she was sure she had never met him. He was not the sort of man a woman forgets.

She regained her slipping poise by tearing her gaze from the stranger's dark face and singing to a table of middle-aged businessmen, clearly having a carefree night on the town before returning to their jobs and their wives.

She wound up the act with a slow, soulful tune pulsing with heartache and lost love. As she finished and bowed to loud applause, she made the mistake of glancing once more at the stranger. His dark eyes held her gaze immobile for an instant and she saw a slight smile curve his firmly sculptured mouth, as if he were aware of a message passing between them.

Urged by the continuing applause to do an encore, she switched to a lighthearted song, putting all she had into it and not looking again at the disturbing man near the stage.

It was a relief to return to her sweltering dressing room. She hoped he wouldn't still be there for her second performance, as he had been the night before. But he was. Irritated by his persistent presence, she ignored him completely and by the time she was well into the act, she had almost forgotten him.

Or she thought she had forgotten him until, upon returning to the dressing room to remove the heavy stage makeup and change into street clothes, she found that she was even more tired than usual after a performance. She attributed this to the effort of will she had expended to dimiss the man's unwavering stare.

She removed her makeup quickly, reapplying a light dusting of powder and pale lip gloss. After hanging the black dress in the narrow makeshift closet, she slipped into the sliver of a sleeveless red silk dress she had worn to work, knotting the tie belt loosely for comfort.

If only her car, which had had an odd little knock in its motor the past couple of days, didn't break down on her way home, she thought wearily. She was stuffing makeup into her black bag when Dirk Cantino walked into the dressing room, leaving the door ajar.

"I remembered you told me you don't eat until after performing, so I'm having the chef send two lobster dinners up to my room. You look as if you could use some nourishment."

His seeming concern did not fool her. She would have walked out immediately, but his tuxedoed form was blocking the door. "I told you earlier, Dirk. I can't make it tonight."

His sangfroid slipped a little. "What is it this time? Expecting a call from your mother? Feel a cold coming on? Or have you thought of another excuse? You're beginning to try my patience, sweetheart. Need I remind you that a word from me and you'll be out on the street?"

"I'm sorry, Dirk, but I have a . . . previous engagement." She attempted to move past him, but he detained her by clasping her arm roughly.

Instantly she became still, sensing that struggling would only make him more aggressive. In his rigid face she saw the effort required for him to stifle his anger. "You're lying, Susan." She still did not move or speak and, finally, a semblance of his usually charming smile erased the frown lines on his forehead. "Okay, honey, I get the message. You want to play hard-to-get. So we'll just have a few drinks and dinner and talk about that job in Vegas. We can at least be friends, can't we?"

"Are you ready, Susan?"

Both Susan and Dirk turned in surprise to see a tall shadowy masculine form looming just behind them in the narrow hall. It was the dark stranger who had watched her with such intensity during her performances the last two evenings.

Dirk scowled at the man and inquired in an aggrieved tone, "Who the hell are you?"

The man offered his hand, but his tone of voice was drawlingly amused. "Travis Sennett."

Dirk muttered his name and shook hands with rude reluctance. "Miss Warren and I have an appointment for dinner," said Travis Sennett, "so if you will excuse us, Cantino . . . ?" For the first time, his glance moved to Susan, who didn't know whether to be grateful or insulted by the man's audacity.

Dirk seemed to be considering objecting, but Travis Sennett's calmly challenging look and superior size evidently made him think better of it. He excused himself curtly and walked stiffly away.

Susan found herself looking up into dark eyes that, as she had already discovered, seemed to be able to probe through her skin and lay her thoughts bare. She felt her face grow warm. "Thank you, Mr. Sennett."

He shrugged. "I heard enough to realize that you needed rescuing."

"I wasn't in any danger," Susan informed him, "but your arrival interrupted what, I'm afraid, might have become quite . . . unpleasant. I have no idea what you're doing here, though. We haven't met before, have we?"

His crooked smile told her he knew that *she* knew they hadn't. "I heard you tell your unwanted Romeo that you had a previous engagement. Do you?"

"No," she admitted. "It seemed the easiest way out of the situation. Actually, I'm dead tired and plan to go straight home."

"I also gathered from what I heard that you haven't had dinner. I would like it very much if you'd have it with me. There's an all-night restaurant not far from here. It's not quite as elegant as the Top Hat, but the food's very good. You have to eat somewhere, and I promise to see you home promptly after the meal."

"I have my car outside." It was the only objection she could think of. To her surprise, the thought of having dinner with this handsome stranger was not unappealing. She did have to eat somewhere, and a meal of scrambled eggs and toast in her tiny apartment didn't seem as appetizing as it had a few minutes earlier.

"No problem," he told her. "I'm from out of town and don't have a car here. We can take yours to the restaurant, after which I'll get a taxi back to the hotel."

"You're staying in *this* hotel?"

He nodded. "Fortunately. Otherwise I might never have heard you sing and come back here to meet you. And we wouldn't be going to dinner together." He smiled disarmingly, strong white teeth flashing in the deep tan of his face. "You are going to say yes, aren't you?"

Susan contemplated the rugged planes of his face with a feeling of wariness. For a moment she just stood there, wondering if she was crazy to be considering going out with Travis Sennett. She suspected that she found him too attractive for her own good. And it wasn't just his admittedly striking physical attributes either; she sensed a strength in him that she had rarely seen in the men who had been, for whatever reason, drawn to her—men like Frank and Dirk.

She knew that she possessed a strength of her own, developed in the five years since she had left college and chosen the difficult, demanding route to becoming a professional singer. Perhaps men like Frank and Dirk had been unconsciously attracted by that strength. But somehow she knew that Travis Sennett wasn't a man who needed to rely on anyone. Rather, he had a confident self-assurance that others would find reassuring, and maybe that was what she found so appealing in him. What would it be like, she wondered fleetingly, to have someone to lean on occasionally?

In the same instant, she told herself that such questions were academic. Travis Sennett would undoubtedly be returning to his home, wherever that was, in a few days. She wouldn't be likely to see him again, so what harm could come of having dinner with him?

"All right," she agreed finally. "I'd like to have dinner with you, Mr. Sennett."

Strong fingers cupped her elbow as they

walked toward the back parking lot entrance. "The name's Travis, Susan."

She flicked a brief glance in his direction as they walked. He was well over six feet; his black hair formed itself attractively to his well-shaped head without aid of dressing or spray. The hair had the mere suggestion of a wave to it as it fell to his collar, thick and gleaming with blue-black highlights under the electric lights in the hall. His cream linen jacket and tan trousers were expensively tailored to a perfect fit. The jacket was open, showing a cream silk shirt tucked into a neat waistband, hinting at the hard, lithe body underneath.

He held the door open for her and she led the way to her four-year-old Chevrolet. She got behind the wheel unhesitatingly, knowing that she didn't need to bolster his ego by asking him to drive. Indeed, she suspected that Travis Sennett's confidence in his masculinity could withstand whatever blows it received and remain unscathed.

He slid into the passenger seat. When she started the engine, it coughed briefly before taking hold. He threw a glance over her as she backed from the parking space. "Shouldn't you have that knock in the motor attended to?"

She left the parking lot and turned in the direction he indicated before replying. "I'm planning to find a mechanic tomorrow." She frowned slightly. "If I'm lucky, it will be something easily fixed—and inexpensive."

He gave her a dry smile. "Sounds rather serious to me. It shouldn't take more than a couple of days to repair, but it could be more costly than you might expect." Apparently, from her job and the age of her car, he had summed up her shaky financial situation rather well.

"Thank you for taking pity on a wayfarer," he remarked, and when she looked his way, gave her a brief crooked smile that held warmth and male allure. "I didn't relish the idea of going to a restaurant alone, and it's too late to order dinner from room service. By the way, you look lovely in that dress."

Susan's smile was ironic. "Thank you, but I'm not going to back out of dinner, so you needn't bother to flatter me."

"I don't say things I don't mean, Susan," he replied calmly. "Nor do I flatter people in an effort to ingratiate myself. I might have lived an easier life if I did." He lounged back against the seat, totally at ease with himself, with her and apparently with her driving. He was certainly a contrast to Frank, who had always been uneasy with women drivers and, in fact, had usually insisted on driving whenever they went anywhere together, even in her car.

Recalling the cramped, uninspiredly drab apartment where she had lived since coming to Miami, she was suddenly glad that she had agreed to have dinner with Travis Sennett. Nevertheless, she had a small nagging suspicion that she might regret it in the morning. But she told herself that was absurd and, for the present, her spirits lifted. She also told herself that it didn't matter that she was deeply conscious of Travis Sennett's lean, muscled body beside her. It was, in fact, somewhat irksome to discover that she was just as aware of him now as she had been earlier that night when he had watched her performance so intently.

All of this she dismissed rather easily as she decided that she didn't regret her decision, in spite of pulses that were leaping rather too quickly. They were ships passing in the night, so why not relax and enjoy her dinner?

The restaurant he had chosen was dimly lit, its atmosphere one of subdued good taste and, in spite of what he had said, clearly expensive. Walking to their table, she was aware of interested glances from men and got an impression of wealth taken-for-granted from the understated elegance of the women's clothing.

She was used to performing in such surroundings, but much less accustomed to being one of the customers. The place was definitely well above her income bracket. Taking the chair the waiter held for her, she lifted her chin high, determined that Travis Sennett should not see the uncertainty in her emerald eyes.

Taking the chair across from her, Travis ran an appraising eye over her. "You put them all in the shade, Susan," he said quietly, startling her. Then he accepted a menu from the waiter and studied it with seeming interest, leaving Susan to recover from her surprise that he had so easily discerned her true feelings. When they had ordered, he said, "So—sultry Susan Warren." He surprised her again by remembering the way she was described on the advertising posters that were scattered about the hotel. "Do you enjoy what you do?"

She fingered her cutlery, her eyes meeting his faintly mocking expression. "It's a living," she told him lightly.

He gazed at her from beneath thick black lashes. "Only a living? I'm sure you don't have to sing for your supper, Susan. An attractive, intelligent young woman like you could find a job in any number of other areas."

"As a matter of fact, my college major was business. I wanted to be able to work in an office if worse came to worst. Singing is a highly precarious business. I've managed to work fairly steadily at it but, goodness knows, I'm not setting the world on fire."

"You're a talented singer, but you sound as if you're rather disillusioned by it all."

She leaned forward slightly and gave in to the urge to unburden herself that Travis Sennett's calmness and strength seemed to elicit in her. "I'm no longer as naive and starry-eyed about the profession as I was five years ago when I left college. I know that I'm passably good as a singer, but good singers are a dime a dozen. If I've learned anything these past five years, it's that it takes a lot more than being able to sing to get to the top."

Travis smiled wryly. "A willingness to be . . . friendly to the likes of Dirk Cantino?"

The creamy tan of her skin grew flushed, but she returned his smile. "Dirk couldn't help my career, even if I encouraged him. But it's no secret that one of the ways for a female performer to get that all-important big chance is by cultivating a man who can give it to her. But there's more to it than that." She spoke seriously. "You have to be relentless. Singing has to be at the top of your list of priorities. And you have to be in the right place at the right time. If I were absolutely driven to succeed, for example, I'd probably be in Nashville or Hollywood now, using all my free time to make the rounds of agents' and producers' offices." Abruptly realizing the absurdity of telling all of this to a stranger, she sat back and concluded on an off-hand note. "Let's just say that the glittering world of show business is looking rather tarnished to me at the moment."

"It appears," he observed thoughtfully, "that you're not prepared to let your career dominate you."

"There are too many other things in life."

Their first course arrived and neither of them spoke while the waiter placed salads and a tray of breads and crackers before them. Susan took a bite of the salad, discovering that the savory house dressing was delicious. "Tell me, Travis," she said after several moments, "do you always eat dinner this late?"

"Not usually," he told her readily. "I didn't eat earlier at the Top Hat because I hoped you would join me later." She looked up quickly and caught his satisfied expression, realizing that he had had little doubt of her acceptance. He really was a confident man, almost irritatingly so.

"Have you lived in Miami long?" he continued smoothly.

"Only four months. I moved here from New Orleans."

"Where you worked as a singer?"

She nodded, and he regarded her meditatively. "I sense that there was more behind the move than a desire to change jobs. Was there a club manager in New Orleans you wanted to escape from?"

Susan responded to the teasing note in the question with a self-conscious smile. "I was engaged and I—*we* decided to call it off. It seemed better all around for me to put some distance between us. And I didn't mean to give you the impression earlier that I don't like Miami. I do, although I wish my job situation wasn't quite as touchy as it is. It's reached the point where I almost expect, every night when I come to work, for Dirk to give me notice. He might have done it tonight if you hadn't interrupted." She lifted her head. "But there are other hotels and supper clubs in town, dozens of them. Anyway, I think Dirk finally knows where I stand, so I shouldn't have anymore trouble with him."

Travis laughed softly. "You don't really believe that, do you? Surely you've seen operators like Cantino before. He won't give up so easily. With him a point of honor is involved—if I may use the term loosely."

"You know," she said, "talking about Dirk Cantino is spoiling my appetite. I'd rather talk about you. Where is your home?"

"Barbados."

"I know it's an island, but I'm a bit unclear about where it's located."

"In the West Indies northeast of Venezuela and directly east, across the Caribbean, from Nicaragua."

"I've never seen the Caribbean, except in

photo stories and on travel posters. It must be a beautiful place."

"The climate and geography are little short of ideal," he agreed, "but, as I'm sure you are aware, the small Caribbean nations have their problems. Barbados is rather unique in that it has a stable government and a healthy economy. Not that we don't have our troubles, too. There are always factions that would like to exploit a country's politics and wealth to their own advantage, and it's usually not in the people's best interests to permit such factions to gain control."

Susan was listening interestedly. "Are you in politics, Travis?"

He smiled. "I'm not an elected official, but I actively support the party that is presently in power. My business is sugar—and banking."

Their main course arrived, but while they busied themselves with the halibut steaks Susan was still thinking about what he had said. "You say part of your business is sugar. Do you grow it?"

"I have a sugarcane plantation, one of the largest on the island. It's been in my family for generations." He continued talking throughout dinner about Barbados and the plantation. It was clear that he loved the place where he lived and the work he did which, from Susan's point of view, placed him among the most fortunate of men. A good many people lived their lives being dissatisfied with one or the other.

When they had finished their after-dinner coffee, he phoned for a taxi for himself, then escorted Susan to her car. The restaurant parking area was sparsely lighted and the shadows playing across the planes of his face emphasized the harsh angularity of his features. Placing a hand on the door handle of her car, Susan turned to say sincerely, "I hope you have an uneventful trip home."

There was a silence. She looked up and found Travis eyeing her, his expression shrouded by shadow. He put a hand out, taking her chin between warm, hard fingers, tipping it back so that his dark eyes could probe her face. "I'll be here a few days longer. Will you have dinner with me again tomorrow night?"

Some feminine instinct warned her to say no, but somehow, with those lancing eyes devouring her features, she couldn't get the words out. Instead, she heard herself saying, "Yes."

She thought he was going to kiss her, and all her senses began to clamor wildly. But he didn't. He continued to survey her flushed face, and then released her chin. "I'll come to your dressing room after the last show."

He stood watching as she started the engine and drove away. Her eyes on the thinning traffic, she turned toward her apartment building. While her hands handled the wheel, her mind simmered with a hodgepodge of reactions.

Susan hadn't reached the age of twenty-six without learning something about men. She had thought herself madly in love at nineteen with a college football player. He had been a playfully amusing boy and their campus romance had ended only when she learned he was vowing eternal devotion to a cheerleader on the nights when he wasn't feeding Susan the same line. A brief infatuation with her English professor in her senior year had been dashed when she discovered, after having dinner with him several times, that he was married and had a son. Faced with an enraged, accusing Susan, he had stated blandly that he hadn't lied to her about it. She contended that, while he may not have lied with words, he had certainly done so with actions and the fact that he had deliberately omitted giving her such a vital bit of information about himself.

These experiences had made her wary of men and entering into any relationship until she was sure of where she stood. Singing jobs had taken her from one place to another with a frequency that prevented her from forming any serious attachments until the job in New Orleans that had lasted eighteen months. After meeting Frank Rosler, she kept her defenses up for a long while, but eventually the persistent little attentions he paid her wore her down. She found that she enjoyed his company and her wariness was so overcome by his charm that she had accepted an engagement ring. Having made the commitment, she tried very hard to overlook Frank's faults. Eventually, though, she had arrived at a point where his considerable charm could no longer outweigh, in her mind, his weakness of character. Cutting her losses, she had left the best job she'd ever had and come to Miami.

From the first moment when she had seen Travis Sennett in the Top Hat, she had sensed the danger he represented. She had known that a woman whose past relationships with men had left her disillusioned and vulnerable would do well to stay away from him. In addition to his physical attractions, of which she was far too aware, there were too many signs of ruthlessness in him—the sensuous mouth that could so quickly form itself into a hard, grim line as it had done when he faced Dirk Cantino, the relentless glint in the dark eyes that had so unsettled her during her act, the cynical expression she had sensed more than seen when he asked her to have dinner with him tomorrow night.

Travis Sennett was a hard man. She was convinced that he could be ruthless in dealing with other men. Could he be as ruthless in his dealings with women?

For the first time she seriously considered the possibility that he might be married. That, at least, was something she must discover during their dinner the next night. Of one thing she was fairly sure: Travis Sennett would not lie to her. He was too cocksure to feel any need for lying.

She was glad he would only be in town a few days. Such a brief acquaintance could surely pose little danger for her. At the same time, she was vexingly aware of something within herself that had flickered into life whenever she set eyes on Travis Sennett. It was irritating to realize that she was disappointed because he hadn't kissed her.

Chapter Three

$\mathcal{U}$ nlocking the door to her apartment, Susan stepped into the small living room followed by Travis Sennett. She switched on the overhead light, exposing the bare off-white walls, the neutral beige of the shag carpet that was beginning to look worn near the door and in front of the olive tweed couch. Susan grimaced in distaste at the room, a replica of a thousand others in apartments throughout the land.

She kept the three small rooms meticulously clean, but the apartment had never seemed quite so drab as it did tonight because she couldn't help imagining how it must look to Travis's eyes. He had talked enough about his home over dinner this evening for her to surmise that it was gracious and steeped in family tradition.

"Make yourself comfortable," she told Travis now, "while I make the coffee."

He tugged the knot of his tie loose. Unfastening the top button of his shirt, he relaxed on the couch, picking up a news magazine from a lamp table. Susan went into the adjoining kitchen. The fact that she had invited Travis to her apartment for coffee after dinner in an intimate little restaurant was just beginning to register fully in her mind. Perhaps the three glasses of wine she had drunk with dinner were to blame, although she was feeling utterly and clearheadedly sober now. She ran water into the pot, measured the coffee and set the glass percolator on the electric range.

While she waited for the coffee to perk, she thought about the evening. True to his word, Travis had appeared at her dressing room minutes after she finished her last performance. As punctual as he was, though, Dirk Cantino was there before him with another plan for Susan to have a drink with him in his room, this one sounding more like a command than his previous invitations.

Dirk hadn't bothered to hide his anger when they were again interrupted by Travis, who had lounged in the doorway and regarded Dirk with steely eyes until Dirk had left. It had been clear to Susan, and evidently to Dirk as well, that Travis was perfectly willing and capable of throwing the manager out bodily if he balked.

"Your boss wasn't very glad to see me," Travis had drawled as he guided Susan to a low-slung blue Trans Am that he had rented for the remainder of his stay in Miami. Susan had left her own car in the garage that morning and it would not be ready for a couple of days. In the meantime, she was using a taxi service for transportation to and from work.

She had passed off her boss's reaction lightly. "I really couldn't care less about that." Inwardly, though, she was troubled by thoughts of how that second confrontation between Dirk and Travis might affect her job.

Nevertheless, she managed to put Dirk and her job out of her mind and enjoy dinner with Travis. He was an interesting conversationalist and an urbane escort. And Susan had to admit to herself that she rather enjoyed the way heads turned when they walked into the restaurant together. Excessive vanity was not one of her faults, but she couldn't help being aware that they made a striking couple.

She had felt more relaxed and talked more animatedly than she could remember doing on a date in a long time. One of the reasons, she knew, that she had allowed herself to respond to Travis so quickly was the knowledge, standing by like a convenient escape hatch, that his return to Barbados was imminent. He had told her tonight that his business in Miami was completed and there had been no indication of anything else that might delay him.

As she entered the living room with their coffee on a tray, Travis's eyes left the magazine and he studied her long, shapely legs as she approached.

Susan set the tray on the low table in front of the couch. "Here we are. You did say you prefer yours black, didn't you?"

"Right," Travis murmured, helping himself to one of the cups. She sat at the other end of the couch and, kicking off her spike-heeled shoes, curled her legs up beneath her tiered lace-trimmed skirt.

Studying her across the width of the couch, he brought up the subject of her boss again. "I hope

I haven't made your situation with Cantino worse than it was already."

"It couldn't be much worse," she told him frankly. "The truth is, I've been thinking of looking for another job." She hadn't been thinking of doing it immediately, but she didn't want him to feel in any way responsible for her problems with Dirk. "I have a friend in New York who's doing well working the big hotels. She's been after me to come for a visit. She can arrange an interview with her agent. Maybe I should go."

After swallowing some of his coffee, he set his cup aside and pulled a thin cheroot from his pocket. "Do you mind if I smoke?" When she shook her head, he produced a gold pocket lighter and drew on the cheroot. He looked at her, his eyes narrowed, the smoke from his cheroot drifting upward. The lines fanning out from his eyes, which she was seeing clearly for the first time, only added to the aura of virility and power that he exuded. "Haven't you any family?" he asked suddenly.

Mercifully, he released her from his riveting gaze. He took another drag on the cheroot and Susan stared into her coffee. "My mother and a brother live in Phoenix. My father died when I was twelve. He was in the insurance business, as is my brother."

"You sound as if you're reading from a resume," he observed wryly.

"I haven't been close to my family since I left college. They've never understood how I could prefer the uncertainty of being a performer to a steady office job." She glanced up at him and laughed softly. "I think my mother suspects I somehow got mixed up with her real daughter in the hospital nursery." Again she was surprised at how easy it was to talk to him. During the two evenings she had spent with him, she had told him more about herself than she ordinarily told people after knowing them for months. But his question about her family gave her the opening she had been looking for all evening.

"It would seem, from what you've said, that your own family is much closer."

His swift glance was sardonic. "I haven't any family, except for an aunt and a couple of cousins in England."

"You—you aren't married?"

"Until the past two years, I worked as a construction engineer in the most primitive corners of the world. There was little time, and even less opportunity for the sort of acquaintanceship that leads to marriage."

"And for the past two years?"

"After I took over my grandfather's business affairs, there was even less time."

"Though more opportunity?" she queried on a slightly breathless note that amazed her. It was startling to discover how glad she was that he didn't have a wife waiting for him on Barbados.

She was disconcerted by the way her question caused him to stare at her unreadably. Then, as if he thought the best defense was an offense, he observed, "We've established that I've been too busy for marriage, but how have you managed to stay unattached for so long?"

He had turned the tables on her, and she flushed under his mocking look. "I suppose I've never found a man I wanted to give up my career for. Singing isn't like most jobs. It requires too much traveling for a marriage to have much of a chance of survival."

"But you told me there was more to life than singing."

Her soft lips curved in a self-deprecating smile. "Which just goes to show that the men I've known haven't exactly bowled me off my feet."

"Not even your ex-fiancé?"

She finished her coffee and set her cup down before she replied. "No." She returned his look steadily. "Oh, I tried to believe for a time that we were right for each other, but eventually I learned that he wasn't the man I had thought. We parted on amicable terms, so probably he had reached the same conclusion about me."

His gaze roamed slowly over her face, as if he were making up his mind about something. "I find that rather hard to believe." He sounded bemused.

She felt a shiver of apprehension go through her. He was like a beautiful wild beast. She was sure he knew things by instinct and could survive in any environment by cunning. Travis Sennett was more man than she'd ever laid eyes on before, and she sensed that in any contest of wills, he would emerge the victor.

He snuffed out his cheroot in an ashtray. As he straightened, the dark eyes narrowed on her face held an intensity of purpose that she had seldom encountered and as they engaged her wide emerald gaze she found that she could not look away. His hand moved up her arm, the dark eyes sliding to her lips then moving down to linger appreciatively on the quickening rise and fall of her breasts beneath the thin white batiste of her blouse.

His other arm came up and he pulled her unresisting body closer to his. For some moments there were no words, for words were unnecessary. Susan had never had a man make love to her with his eyes before, but it was happening now as his gaze moved slowly from the pulse pounding in her throat over her slightly parted lips, her glowing emerald eyes, the smoothness of her brow. Her senses responded as turbulently as if he were touching her with caressing fingers rather than with a look. Then his hand reached up to stroke the silver sheen of her hair, smoothing the cascading waves away from her face.

"You have beautiful hair." It was almost a casual observation, as if he had remarked upon the beauty of a fine piece of porcelain.

The fingers that had touched her hair examined the line of her cheek and jaw. His hand felt warm and hard, and she wondered dazedly how anything so hard could be so gentle. Then his fingers cupped themselves lightly against her throat, lifting her chin. His mouth came down to taste her soft lips and with gentle persuasion he parted them to slowly and thoroughly explore their sweetness. As if some irresistible magnetic force were at work, her mouth clung to his.

Finally, reluctantly, he lifted his head. Her eyes, touched with a slumberous gaze, came open. His look was momentarily confused and then quickly veiled.

"Susan?" His tone held some of the bewilderment she had glimpsed in his eyes. He seemed to be holding himself tightly in check, and at the same time debating something with himself. Finally, he said, "I'm leaving the day after tomorrow. Will you have dinner with me again tomorrow night?"

She nodded wordlessly, unable to so quickly shake the confusion she felt, as if the mystification she had glimpsed so briefly in his eyes had communicated itself to her. She felt so weak and compliant, as if she had no will to disagree with whatever he said. She knew that he sensed her dazed state, and any other man would have been quick to take advantage of it. For reasons of his own, which Susan could not begin to guess, he did not.

His sudden withdrawal was at once a disappointment and a reprieve. He got to his feet.

"Until tomorrow."

"Good night, Travis," she whispered as he strode across the room and let himself out.

Dirk Cantino was waiting in her dressing room when she arrived at work the next evening.

"I've been in touch with my contact in Vegas," he told her as she slipped the powder blue strapless gown she would wear for her performance from a hanger. "I should know definitely next week if I'm in. I won't be going out there until winter, though. The man whose place I'll be taking is holding them to their contract and won't clear out until then."

"I see," Susan responded noncommittally. She didn't feel up to trying to bolster Dirk's ego by saying she knew he'd get the job. Evidently he didn't feel much like pretending, either, for his usually ready charm had been lacking in the straightforward speech. Susan was grateful. She much preferred a businesslike approach from her boss to a more familiar one.

Now he said, "I spoke to them about you. We can talk about terms tonight after your last show."

She draped the blue gown over a folding screen, not looking at him. "That won't be possible. I'm seeing Travis Sennett again tonight."

Dirk's anger flared. "Where in thunder did that dude come from?"

"Barbados," Susan told him simply.

"How long have you known him?"

She didn't appreciate the proprietary demand in his question. "Awhile."

He faced her squarely, his jaw tight. "Let me spell it out for you, sweetheart. I can help you or I can hurt you. It's up to you."

Susan stared at him with feigned innocence. "Isn't my act satisfactory?"

He made a contemptuous sound. "I could leave here right now and, within an hour, find a dozen singers who would do anything to have your job, and probably sing just as well."

"I didn't realize," responded Susan calmly, "there were so many unemployed singers in Miami."

"Let's stop the sparring, shall we? Will you

meet me tonight after the show? And you'd better be prepared to be much friendlier than you've been up to now."

"I've already told you. I am otherwise engaged."

He stared at her for a long moment, his jaw working violently. "Then I have a bulletin for you, Susan. We won't be needing your services after the end of the month." He turned on his heel and slammed out of the dressing room.

Susan watched him go with her mouth open. It wasn't as if she hadn't been expecting an ultimatum, but she realized now that she had thought Dirk was prepared to be more patient. She had even imagined that he might be enjoying the pursuit a little.

She raked her fingers disconsolately through her long hair. It hardly seemed to make a great difference whether she was out of a job at the end of the month or a few months down the line. Sooner or later, she would have found herself in this predicament, for she had never given an instant's consideration to capitulating to Dirk's outrageous demands. She wouldn't be blackmailed by the biggest producer in Hollywood, much less by a small time semihood like Dirk Cantino! She should have said that to him, she told herself furiously. But, no, she thought with a heavy sigh, what would be gained by making her remaining days at the Top Hat more uncomfortable than they already would be as things stood now?

After being given her notice, she wasn't psychologically at her best during her act that evening, but she got through it. And she must have managed to keep her anxiety well enough hidden, for Jacky didn't seem to suspect that she was troubled and the crowd demanded encores at both performances.

The effort required, however, was enough to make her feel exhausted by the time Travis arrived at her dressing room to take her to dinner. She had changed into a simply cut dress of cherry-colored summer crepe with the mere suggestion of sleeves, a deeply v'ed roll collar and large buttons down the front. When Travis knocked she had been sitting in the wicker chair with her chin in one hand and her eyes closed for perhaps five minutes.

Opening the door, she managed what she hoped was a perky smile for Travis, who looked devastatingly handsome in a suit of summer white.

"What?" he drawled laconically as his gaze scanned the dressing room. "Don't I get to show your boss the door again?"

"You're too late, I'm afraid. He was here before the first performance."

He regarded her gravely. "Oh? Did he give you any trouble?"

"Nothing I couldn't handle," Susan said. "Shall we go? I'm famished."

She was determined not to let the loss of her job spoil this last evening with Travis, and so she stiffened her spine and chatted about inconsequential things on the drive and all through dinner. She suspected, though, that he was not entirely fooled. More than once, she looked up to see him studying her in a very deliberative way.

As they were having dessert, he said, "You

seem tired this evening. There's a look of strain in your eyes. Aren't you sleeping well?"

"When I go to bed, I die," she reassured him. "I've always been like that. The world could be teetering on the brink of collapse, and I probably wouldn't lose much sleep over it." She finished her sherbet and smiled at him.

"Is your world teetering, Susan?" he asked quietly.

His transfixing gaze was almost too much for her, and her smile died. "Travis Sennett," she said with a little shrug, "didn't your mother ever tell you not to ask ladies such personal questions?"

There was a slight hardening of the planes of his face but otherwise his expression was inscrutable. "My mother walked out on me when I was ten."

Somehow the straightforward way he said it made the words strike Susan with staggering force. "Oh, Travis, I'm sorry. I had no idea—I didn't mean anything by that remark."

He continued to regard her with solemnity. "I know you didn't. How could you? Forget it. I have. I hardly remember what she looked like."

Susan would have had no doubt that he meant it if she hadn't seen the subtle change in his face at the mention of his mother. She sensed that they were on unsafe ground and changed the subject abruptly.

"That was a lovely dinner."

He nodded. "It was rather good, wasn't it? There are so many excellent restaurants in this town. I'd suggest we order more coffee, but I think I'd better get you home."

In the car, she settled back and relaxed against the plush blue upholstery as the Trans Am moved smoothly into the street, its engine purring softly. Travis threw an oblique glance over her and gave her a brief, crooked smile. She was deeply conscious of his body beside her, but for some reason she no longer felt the need to stave off silence. She put her head back and closed her eyes and they made the drive to her apartment with little conversation.

At her door, Travis said, "Are you going to invite me in?"

She looked up at him, aware of the profound impact his nearness was having on her pulses, but she succeeded in making her voice calm and casual. "If you like." When they were inside, she tossed her purse into a chair, saying, "I'll put some coffee on."

She had reached the kitchen door when his voice detained her. "Susan." She turned around questioningly. "It's not coffee that I want." His face held little expression, but there was a veiled question in his dark eyes.

He came slowly toward her. She looked up at him, her eyes widening slightly. Her heart was racing madly. His hands settled lightly on her shoulders to pull her close to him, then moved to gently caress her bare arms. Her eyes closed flutteringly. His touch was the same peculiar combination of roughness and tenderness that had so surprised and pleased her the night before.

His breath was warm against her brow and she opened her eyes just before his mouth took hers in a long, intoxicating kiss. She ran her hands tentatively over his iron-muscled upper arms, aware that his fingers were slowly undoing the buttons of her dress.

He paused in his endeavor when his hands discovered the swelling fullness of her breasts in the lacy wisp of a bra she wore. She tasted the wine that he had drunk with dinner and smelled the faint fragrance of cheroot. His maleness assailed all her senses, drugging her.

An exploring finger slowly followed the outline of the hardening tip of one breast, and a weakness such as she had never known took possession of her legs. She swayed against him and his arms suddenly encircled her like steel bands and crushed her against him, surrounding her with hardness and a heat that quickly communicated itself to her own flesh.

He lifted his head long enough to look into her eyes and what he saw there caused a sharp intake of breath. His mouth traveled over the soft curve of her cheek, sought out the sensitive spot below her earlobe then continued down the silken smoothness of her neck.

His tongue flicked sensuously into the hollow at the base of her throat where a pulse jerked crazily. By the time his mouth returned to savor her lips again, she was quaking with sensations that had lain dormant for a long time. The lazy sensuality of his kiss built a fire inside her, and with a will of its own, her body arched and shaped itself to his.

With a soft moan, he lifted her as easily as he might have lifted a child and carried her to the bedroom. Susan lay in a languorous daze as he undressed her, her body totally compliant. Dark lashes fluttered down and she watched through their fringes as he shrugged out of his clothes with an easy litheness.

Then she was covered by the solid, warm length of his naked body. She locked her arms around the bronze hardness of his neck and lifted her soft mouth eagerly for his plundering kiss.

He made love to her with a deliberate slowness, keeping the boiling passion in himself within rigid bounds until she was brought to a sensuous arousal that was overwhelming in its need. No man had ever made her feel like this before. Raging fire and unbearable tension built inside her until her fingernails were digging into the rippling muscles of his back, and her body was arching against him in a plea for release.

His desire burst its bounds then and his thrusting body answered her unspoken plea with the same deliberate slowness that took her higher and higher, to the brink of human sensation, lifting her, lifting her with him until she plunged over the edge in a shattering explosion of feeling that vibrated in the very depths of her soul.

Chapter Four

Sunlight trickled through an opening in the coarsely textured curtains and settled in a golden puddle on one side of Travis's sleeping face. Susan stirred languidly and turned her head on the pillow to look at him. The night just past now seemed only a misty phantasm, but the solid bulk of him beside her, the sheet a snowy contrast to the dark hair springing from the taut, tanned skin of his chest, assured her that she had not dreamed it.

Her eyes took in the thick tousle of black hair, the wide forehead, the heavy brows and lashes, the strong nose and dark-stubbled chin, the prominent cheekbones with the slight hollows beneath. The virile beauty of him filled her senses and made her breath lodge in her throat. The feelings the slow appraisal stirred in her were too lovely to resist, and she touched his cheek with tenderness, smoothed the disordered strands of hair back from his forehead.

He murmured an incoherent guttural sound, and a smile touched the sensuous outline of his mouth. His lids came open slowly and slumberous gold-glinted brown eyes looked into hers.

"What time is it?"

"I don't know. Very late, I think." Her hand shifted to his hard chest, the fingers working themselves slowly in among the curling black hairs. She wanted to touch him everywhere, to trace the outlines of the body that she had learned during the night so that its imprint would be impressed into her fingers and palms as it was burned in her brain. The knowledge that very soon he would walk out of her life and she would never see him again was a leaden weight in her chest. "What time does your plane leave?"

His eyes traveled lingeringly down the smooth curve of her cheek, over the ivory satin skin of her neck and shoulders to the soft mounds of her breasts half-covered by the sheet. He tugged at the sheet, exposing her, and she saw the slumbering passion in his dark eyes glow and catch fire. His hand molded itself to her rib cage and he buried his face in the cavity between her breasts, burrowing sensuously with his tongue.

"What plane?" The husky words were muffled by the burgeoning fullness of her flesh, and his breath heated her skin deliciously.

She placed both hands on his head, her fingers entangled in his hair, and pressed him into her with a soft sigh. "Oh, Travis—Travis."

He was brushing her with his lips and his wondrous strong and gentle hands, and her pores were coming to life under his touch, opening and quivering with melting warmth.

"You are too beautiful to be real," he said thickly as he lifted her to lie on top of him. She felt the firm length of his thighs, the pulsing hardness of his desire and the way her soft breasts were crushed against the solid roughness of his chest.

Her hair was a curtain of silvery blondness enclosing their faces as she looked deeply into the musteline depths of his eyes. She lowered her lips to his, touching gently at first, tracing the warm contours with the moist tip of her tongue. He groaned, the intimate warmth of his breath entering her mouth, and his arms tightened around her, pulling her harder against him as if he wanted her body to meld into his, to be a part of him. The kiss deepened, and his hands moved over her back and the curve of her hips to lift and press her even closer, and finally, easily, the ultimate closeness was accomplished.

Their bodies were moist with the mingled heat of their desire. Susan wanted to wait, to draw out and savor the sweet spasms that were filling her. He was a part of her and all around her, and she wanted it never to end. But she couldn't stop the pressure that was building in both of them as they moved together in the perfect rhythm of love. She felt as if all of her life had been leading up to this one shattering moment when her yielding softness became one with the unleashed power of this man.

There was a moment of suspended stillness, a moment out of time, and then with a plunging feeling all else was drowned in an overwhelming rush of sensation that was like the sun exploding, the melting of the elements.

"Susan!" Her name sounded as if it had been torn from the deepest well of his being. Then, more quietly, unsteadily, "Ah, Susan . . ."

They lay still, their bodies entwined, their eyes closed as their labored breathing slowed. After a few moments, he settled her against his side with her head tucked under his chin, and one leg lying across both of his. They lay together like interlocking pieces of a puzzle as his hand moved down the length of her back, molding her closer.

"You have filled me and drained me all at the same time," he whispered softly. He pressed his lips against her forehead and with gentle fingers smoothed back the moist tangle of her hair.

She wrapped an arm and a leg around him and pressed her face into his neck, inhaling the musky masculinity of his skin. She felt his body relaxing and heard the measured slowness of his breathing and thought that he had fallen asleep. She lay very still so as not to awaken him. When he awoke he would leave. He would leave—oh, please, no. . . .

A wave of wrenching sadness rose in her and she pressed her eyelids tightly closed for long moments to keep back the hot tears. It wasn't until he spoke that she knew he hadn't been asleep at all. Even then she believed briefly that *she* had fallen asleep, must surely be dreaming.

"Marry me, Susan."

At first she did not move, did not want to dispel the dream. She felt the warm sunlight on her body, saw the blank whiteness of the far bedroom wall through the dark screen of her lashes, and comprehension uncurled in her. She lifted her head and looked into his face, a frown of disbelief knitting her brow.

"What did you say?"

A slow smile lifted a corner of his mouth, partially exposed the even line of white teeth. "I asked you to marry me."

She sat up abruptly, tugging at the sheet and tucking it tightly around her at her armpits, succeeding at the same time in draping one end of it over him below the waist.

She managed a shaky laugh. "You have a weird sense of humor, you know that?"

"I'm not joking."

"But you can't *mean* it."

He lifted his head to support it on one hand and looked at her. "Of course I mean it."

She stared at him, searched for a hint of teasing in his expression, but could find none. "We—we don't even know each other very well."

A devilish glint flashed in his eyes. "We know all the important things." A muscle at one corner of his mouth twitched. "Oh, I get it. You don't respect me anymore."

There was no hope of being reasonable while he was so close to her, teasing and looking at her like that. She left the bed, taking the sheet with her and clutching it about her. Suddenly she felt as if she needed its protection.

He lay back, arms behind his head, unabashedly naked, and laughed at her. "Isn't it a little late for modesty?"

"I can't think when I'm . . . uncovered."

He watched her, amused, as she wrapped the sheet more carefully about herself and tried to comb some of the disorder out of her hair with her fingers. Finally she met his look and said gravely, "I'm going to take a shower. I—I want you to know—I'm aware that a person might say

66

things he doesn't really mean when he's feeling
. . . close to someone and . . . vulnerable. I'll understand if you're gone when I come back." She
turned away from him and padded across the
carpet, a corner of the sheet dragging behind
her like a train.

In the bathroom, she turned on the shower,
adjusting it to a warm, hard spray before she
stepped in. She just stood for several moments,
letting the water hit her with its force and run off
her in streams. Gradually, her body began to
relax and she felt slightly calmer. But her mind
continued to go in circles.

The mere thought of becoming Travis's wife,
of going with him to Barbados and repeating the
experiences of last night again and again, made
her feel weak with longing. But the well-
developed sensible side of her nature reminded
her that sex—even the dazzlingly glorious sort
she'd shared with Travis—was not enough to
make a marriage work. She was insightful
enough, too, to realize that her own unhappy
situation in Miami might be bathing the experiences of the last few days in a rosy glow that
would dissipate in the mundane every-dayness
of married life.

These thoughts did not keep her imagination
from veering off into wonderful daydreams of
life as Mrs. Travis Sennett, though. But all this
confusion was probably academic, anyway, she
told herself scornfully as she turned her back to
the spray and let it drench her hair.

Travis would undoubtedly have had second
thoughts by the time she emerged. Even now he
was probably scrambling into his clothes, thank-

ing his lucky stars she'd seen fit to offer him a graceful way out of his impetuous proposal. He would be gone when she returned to the bedroom, and she would never see him again. She made herself face that, but the thought caused a sharp pain in her midsection that made her gasp and she had to swallow several times to fight down the nausea that rose in her throat.

She stayed in the shower for a long time and, when she emerged to dry her body and wrap her dripping hair in a towel, turban-style, she made herself linger for more long minutes to give him ample time to vacate the apartment.

Finally she lifted her white terry robe from a hook on the door and slipped it on over skin that tingled and glowed pink from the sharp shower spray. She lapped the robe in front and tied the belt snugly. She put her hand on the doorknob and drew several long breaths, steeling herself to face the emptiness of the apartment.

When she stepped into the bedroom, Travis was sitting on the edge of the bed in his trousers and shirt, smoking a cheroot. He raked her with a thoughtful scrutiny before he said, "Do you always take so long in the shower?"

The sight of him sitting there, solid and real, set off a speeded up drumming of her heart. "I wanted to give you plenty of time to get dressed and go."

"Not until I get an answer to my question."

She clutched at the lapels of her robe, pulling them more closely together. "I—I don't know what to say, Travis. It seems too fast. I don't want you to rush into anything you'll regret later. Also—" She swallowed but made herself go on. "I think you should know that I've lost my job. I'm in a pretty precarious position right now. If I said yes, it would be only natural if you thought I was marrying you because of that."

"Would you be?"

His dark eyes held hers gravely. She shook her head. "No," she said in a tone that was barely above a whisper. "I wouldn't do that. It might not be easy, but I can get another job. I've no doubt of it."

"Assuming that you are considering saying yes," he went on, still holding her eyes with his as he stubbed out the cheroot in an ashtray on the bedside table, "what *are* your reasons?"

After a long moment, she said falteringly, "You're an extremely attractive man, Travis Sennett. I think we both know that last night was very special." She paused, seeing the fathomless deepening of the brown eyes. She wanted desperately to say what she was beginning to suspect, that already she was falling in love with him. But it seemed so incredible, so unlike her to fall in love with a man she'd known only a few days. Yet hardly as incredible, she thought dazedly, was the fact that she was actually considering marrying him—yes, wanted to marry him at this moment as she had never wanted anything before in her life, and hang the consequences.

He took a long breath and got to his feet. Coming to her, he touched her cheek tentatively. "Then I'll ask you again. Will you marry me?"

She looked into his face, feeling bemused. She knew that all the statistics were against such a hasty marriage, that she might very well come to regret it. But she also knew that she wanted nothing so much as to go with him when he left Miami, to be with him all the time.

"It's impulsive and probably crazy." She hesitated, seeing the hopeful expectancy in his expression, as if her acceptance were truly vital to him. She thought of asking him to stay in Miami longer so that they could spend more time together before taking such a drastic step. But instead, she said, "Yes, I'll marry you. Oh, yes."

Slowly, deliberately, he pulled her into his arms and his lips covered hers. The kiss was deep and probing, drawn out and filled with bittersweet hunger. Finally, he tore his mouth from hers with a reluctant sound and set her away from him. "If we don't stop this, we'll spend the rest of the day in bed." His eyes burned with the desire unleashed by the kiss. "Much as I want that, there are things I must do." He ran a hand over the rough overnight growth of beard on his chin. "I'll go back to the hotel and shower and shave. Then I'll see about the license and blood tests, and get us on a flight to Barbados tomorrow or the next day—as soon as everything can be arranged." He gripped her shoulders again and kissed her quickly with hard possession, then let her go abruptly. "I'll be back as soon as it's all set." His look was solemn all at once. "You won't change your mind, will you?"

A foolish question, she thought and smiled. "No."

He smiled, too, and left the apartment after looking back once to brush her with his eyes.

When he was gone, Susan's knees felt suddenly weak. She lowered herself to the side of the bed, loosened the towel and began drying her hair with it. After a moment, she stopped and stared at the doorway through which Travis had just passed. If she had a friend who was about to do what she was doing, she would do everything in her power to convince that friend to wait awhile. It was every kind of insanity to be planning to marry Travis in a day or two. There were so many arguments against it. And what was there in favor of it, really? Only her utter certainty that there would never be another man like Travis for her. Knowing this, she couldn't bear to let him walk out of her life.

Susan spent the day preparing for the trip to Barbados. After several phone calls, she finally located her landlord and told him she was moving. Since she hadn't given notice, she had to forfeit the month's rent she'd paid a few days earlier. Then she called the mechanic who was repairing her car and arranged with him to sell it for whatever he could get and send her the money, minus a commission.

Then she called Dirk at the hotel, and thoroughly enjoyed telling him that she was leaving her job immediately.

"Come on, honey," he responded, his voice laced with disbelieving contempt, "you really can't afford this grand gesture, can you? Besides, you know I can't get another singer by tonight."

"But I thought you could just walk out on the

street and find a dozen," Susan told him. "If not, I guess you'll have to fill in yourself. How's your singing voice, Dirk?"

"Be here for the first show tonight!" he said, all the drawl gone from his voice now. "Or you won't get a penny's vacation or severance pay."

"I'm awfully sorry," she said sweetly, "but I just can't make it."

He uttered a string of curses, several of which she'd never even heard before. "You'll live to regret this, Susan. I'll blacken your name from here to Las Vegas. It'll be a long time before you sing professionally again."

She sighed elaborately. "Well, that's the way the cookie crumbles, I guess. Besides, I'm getting married and leaving the country, so I doubt that I'll have much time for singing in the near future. Give my regards to Jacky, will you? Oh, and good luck with your singing debut tonight. I really regret that I'll be too busy to come and hear it." She dropped the receiver into the cradle in the middle of another string of uncomplimentary epithets.

Four days later Susan was Mrs. Travis Sennett and sitting beside her husband on a plane bound for Barbados. Those four days had run together in her mind until she couldn't distinguish one from the other. She had phoned her mother in Phoenix with the news and promised to write all the details later. Her mother had congratulated her but, as usual, had questioned the wisdom of what Susan was doing—in this case, going to live so far away in a place that, when all was said and done, was really a foreign country. Wisely, Susan refrained from telling her that she'd barely known Travis a week. That would certainly have given her mother something to criticize. But she was too happy for her mother's negativism to affect her.

There had been several phone calls and trips to the visa office and the consulate, for she had wanted to make sure of what she would have to do to establish dual citizenship and permanent residency in Barbados. Although Travis had assured her that there would be no problems with either, she had felt better talking to the proper authorities herself and going through all the recommended steps.

She had spent one entire day shopping for her wedding dress and squandered most of her savings on it. But it was worth it, she told herself now, as she smoothed her hands along the pale lilac silk from waist to knees, then gently touched the giant orchid corsage that Travis had given her. She was also wearing new pearl-white sling pumps with a matching bag. Travis had wanted to pay for the outfit, but, again, she had insisted upon doing it herself.

"I think," he had commented dryly, "that I'm marrying an independent woman."

He had contented himself with taking her to the poshest jewelry store she'd ever seen and letting her choose the rings—wide platinum bands with four good-sized diamonds in hers and a modest solitaire in his. When she had made her choice, Travis had grinned and said teasingly, "You have exquisite taste, darling."

She hadn't asked what the rings had cost; she hadn't wanted to know.

That had been yesterday, and this morning they had stood before a judge who pronounced them husband and wife. It still seemed like something that had happened only in her imagination, and she turned her head to look at Travis, to assure herself that he was real. He had pushed his seat back after takeoff and sprawled beside her, as much as it was possible to sprawl in an airplane seat, with his eyes closed.

A soft smile touched her lips. He seemed more ruggedly handsome to her every time she looked at him. And she no longer had any doubts about whether she was in love. Dear heaven, she adored him—desperately, maybe even obsessively. He was an addiction, a fever in her blood.

Unable to resist touching him, she put her hand over his, where it rested on his knee. He opened his eyes to meet her gaze and smiled.

"I didn't mean to wake you."

He adjusted his seat. "You didn't. I can never sleep in these cramped quarters." He turned his hand palm up to clasp hers and squeezed gently.

She laughed. "Gracious, I feel as if I can spread out in all directions. I've never traveled first class before."

"It beats coach, I'll admit. What I'd really like, though, is to have a private room all to ourselves." His tone was teasingly erotic. "So that I could have my way with you."

She looked into his eyes for a long moment and felt her pulse leap. "Stop looking at me like that," she said with a slight breathlessness.

He bent to kiss her forehead. "You're right. I think we'd better turn this conversation to other things."

"Tell me about Barbados. I want to know everything. Were the British the first people to live there?"

"No, not by more than two thousand years. Several early Indian tribes beat them to it. The last were the Caribs, who were very fierce and loved war, and they killed or conquered the others, or drove them off the island. 'Carib' comes from the Spanish word for cannibal, which they were."

"What happened to them?"

"Spanish and Portuguese ships began to stop at the island."

"Did the Caribs eat them?" Susan asked, shuddering.

"A few, but they were no match for the Europeans' superior weapons or for the smallpox and other diseases they brought. The Indians who didn't die in battle or from disease were probably transported as slaves to Spanish colonies."

"It's ironic, isn't it? The Caribs suffered the same fate they visited on their Indian enemies. They might not have been served for dinner, but they might have preferred that to slavery."

"It's the way of all human history. The strong conquer the weak." The blunt statement intruded into her blissful happiness, but only briefly. Travis continued, "The first English settlers came to the island about a hundred years after the Caribs disappeared. It was a rigorous life, but they planted crops that did well in the tropical climate and the settlement grew. The first Sennett arrived before 1700. My plantation has been in the family ever since. Eventually sugarcane arrived and Barbados evolved into a slave society, with Africans being brought to work on the plantations. The slaves were emancipated in the 1830's and we've been an independent nation since 1966."

"Then your government is parliamentary, patterned on England's?"

He stroked her fingers idly as he nodded. "I think I told you that my party is presently in power. There's a strong opposition party, as well, but most members of both major parties have the best interests of Barbados at heart."

"You said something once about a group of people who want to exploit the island."

Two frown lines etched themselves between his dark brows. "I'm sure there are that kind in every country. Our would-be exploiters are relatively small in number, but they're powerful because the leaders seem to have wealth and influence. They keep a low profile, naturally. Nobody seems to know for certain exactly who the leaders are, but we all have our suspicions." There was a hard, grim set to his mouth. "They're nothing but petty tyrants who would like to turn the island into a dictatorship and bleed it dry."

Susan felt a small stab of alarm. "Is there any danger of that happening?"

"Not as long as I, and all the people like me who want representative government, stay alert and take nothing for granted." He glanced at her and saw her worried expression. His face cleared and he chuckled. "Don't give it another thought. I tend to get carried away when I think about what those people are trying to do, but there's really no danger of it coming about. We have our problems, but most of them have little to do with politics."

"It must have been nice growing up there," Susan murmured after a moment. "I'll bet you know everyone on the island."

"Almost everyone. Many of the friends I grew up with stayed on the island or returned after moving away for a while, as I did. One friend who I want you to meet is Kay Harte, who was a classmate of mine until I went away to college. She runs a boutique in Bridgetown, where you'll probably be doing a lot of shopping. She keeps up with the fashion trends in Paris and New York and has one of the best selections of women's clothing on Barbados. I want you to have female friends."

She gave him an impish smile. "But no male ones? Tell me, was Kay your teen-age sweetheart?"

His expression was amused. "No. We were together a lot, growing up, but we were never more than friends."

"Good," she said contentedly. "Then I won't need to be jealous of her."

"You don't need to be jealous of anyone, my darling," he said with a look that sent a delicious shiver up her backbone. A sudden image of the children she and Travis might someday have together flashed into her mind.

"You're looking rather pleased with yourself," Travis told her. "What were you thinking just then?"

"I don't want to give you any more ideas at the moment than you already have," she teased.

"Tell me, woman," he ordered.

She brought his hand to her mouth, brushing the fingers with her lips. "I was thinking about our future children." She looked up at him. "I hope you want children. I just realized we've never discussed it."

"I want *your* children very much," he assured her, his dark eyes caressing her face. "And the sooner the better. I'm not getting any younger, and I want to watch them grow up."

"By all means," she said with a tinkling laugh. "Since you're already such a tottering old gentleman, we'd better waste no time—once we're off this plane," she added as his hand came to rest on her thigh.

"I want you now," he said unnecessarily.

"I know, love," she responded softly, "but we mustn't shock that elderly lady across the aisle. Try to get some sleep, why don't you?"

"Fat chance," he growled, "with you sitting there looking so beautiful."

But he pushed his seat back again and closed his eyes, and Susan followed his example. She didn't doze, however. Her mind was too busy wondering what Barbados and Travis's plantation would be like. Would his friends, Kay Harte, for instance, approve of her? It was odd that, as much as Travis seemed to want a family, he hadn't married before now, in spite of what he'd told her about being too busy with his work. She knew there must have been a number of women in his life before she met him. Ah, well, she thought placidly, she must thank her luck that he'd stayed single and apparently uncommitted to any other woman before her, for whatever reason.

The flight finally came to an end, and Susan waited with their luggage outside the terminal while Travis claimed his French-made sports car, which he had left in the airport parking lot, and brought it around. They drove along a narrow road past green hills and cultivated plots of sugarcane and yams with the brilliant blue sea never out of sight. It was as lovely as Susan had imagined, and she gazed raptly through the car window the whole way, trying to take in everything.

There was too much, of course. She could hardly wait until she could take the car and explore the island on her own while Travis worked the long hours he had warned her about.

Evening was coming on as they passed through the narrow, bustling main street of Bridgetown at a snail's pace. Travis pointed out the bank in which he held the controlling interest. It was a large gray structure rising three stories from the street. Along the second floor in front ran a roofed veranda with white wrought-iron columns and railing. Above the third story, two square towers rose, their rounded domes also painted white. The building was impressive and added to Susan's rapidly growing certainty that she had married an extremely wealthy man.

Turning off the main street, they passed Trafalgar Square, with Lord Nelson's statue at its center, and the Careenage, a basin used mainly, Travis said, by the quaint and colorful interisland schooners and motor vessels.

"Careenage." Susan repeated the word. "I've never heard that term before. What does it mean?"

"It's French, from 'careened,' which means to tilt a ship far enough over so that the bottom can be cleaned."

Soon they were in the countryside again and turning down a drive crisscrossed with the long shadows of the palm trees bordering it on both sides. From the little Travis had told her, Susan had expected something large, but she was not prepared for the picture-book graciousness of the old plantation house that sprawled ahead of them. Its white walls were dazzling in the last of the day's sunlight; green awnings and a red roof added bold touches. There was a circular section at the center with rectangular wings extending on either side. The large lawn in which the house sat was carpet smooth and meticulously tended.

"Travis!" Susan gasped. "Why didn't you warn me that it was so grand?"

He chuckled. "Words can't do it justice. But you'll soon discover that it isn't as perfect as it looks. The plumbing is ancient, for one thing. We'll have to have it replaced within the next year or two, I'm afraid." He grimaced. "It'll cost a fortune. We're always fighting to keep ahead of leaks in the roof, too, during the rainy season. This roof's only five years old, but there are so many eaves and angles that it's difficult to make it completely waterproof. The furniture's old, and some of it was very inexpensive even when it was new. Most of it's solidly built, though, and we'll replace it with pieces that you want as we can afford it."

"Who cares about plumbing and roofs and furniture?" Susan said. "It's beautiful and I love it."

He gave her a grateful look. "So do I," he said with a note of earnestness in his voice.

They were greeted by a small, round-faced black woman whom Travis introduced as Mala. Mala was accompanied by a younger version of herself, who turned out to be her daughter, Amii.

Both women were frankly amazed to discover that their employer had returned home with a wife. "How come you not tell me you gettin' married?" Mala demanded in an aggrieved tone.

"There wasn't time," Travis said. "It happened too fast."

"This not like you," Mala commented, studying Susan with an expression that clearly reserved judgment on what kind of wife she would make. "You always rush, rush to work—but not with the women."

"I'd better warn you," Travis said to Susan with a twinkle in his eyes, "that Mala is the real boss around here, and she doesn't like surprises much."

"Not two big ones all at once, for sure," Mala said.

"There's another one?" Travis inquired.

Mala nodded solemnly. "We got company.

Your cousins from England show up early this mornin' and say they wait for you."

"Curt and Violet?" All the lighthearted banter was gone from Travis's voice suddenly. "Damnation! They couldn't have picked a worse time for a visit. Where are they?"

"On the back veranda, las' I knew," Mala said, "drinking up all our rum."

Grim-faced, Travis strode quickly toward the back of the house. After looking questioningly at the closed faces of the two black women, Susan followed him.

Chapter Five

𝒯he impression she got in her hurried journey through the house was one of large rooms and dark furniture, but she was too intent on keeping Travis in sight to pay close attention.

She caught up with him in the kitchen and followed him through an open door onto a wide veranda overlooking more well-tended lawn. Two people sat in wrought-iron patio chairs with a small, round table between them. There were several empty liquor glasses on the table. The couple heard their approach and both of them looked up at the same moment and got to their feet.

The man was almost as tall as Travis but not as well muscled. He was about thirty, with narrow shoulders, light brown hair, a thin mouth and a receding chin that gave him a look of weakness. He was smoking a cigarette in a long ivory holder.

The woman appeared to be a year or two younger than the man. She had thick red hair and green eyes and although she had applied her makeup with a too-generous hand she was pretty in a brittle sort of way. Both of the visitors had first looked at Travis and then, startled, at Susan.

The woman recovered first and stepped forward to give Travis an obviously unwelcome hug. "Travis, darling! How wonderful to see you again. We were crushed when we arrived and learned you were away."

Travis extricated himself from the woman's arms and said tensely, "Hello, Violet. And Curt." He drew Susan to his side. "Darling, these are my cousins, Violet Graves and Curt Winston. Violet, Curt, I'd like you to meet my wife, Susan."

Violet appeared to be struck momentarily dumb, but Curt extended a hand that felt soft in Susan's grip. "Well!" Curt said with a heartiness that sounded forced. "This *is* a surprise. We had no idea, Travis, not that I can blame you now that I've seen her." He smiled at Susan. "How long have you and Travis known each other?"

"Long enough," put in Travis tersely. Susan glanced up at him uncertainly. It was obvious that he disliked these cousins of his intensely. She decided to keep her distance from them until she learned more about the background of that dislike.

"You both have our congratulations," Curt was saying.

"Thank you," Susan murmured.

Violet spoke. "Mala didn't see fit to tell us you were married."

"My employees don't discuss my business with others," Travis said in the same tense tone he'd used with Curt.

Violet's painted lips curved in a smile that

didn't soften the glitter in her green eyes, a glitter that looked to Susan very much like anger. There were undercurrents here that she couldn't begin to fathom.

"How odd that you should put your marriage in the category of business," the woman said, her gaze slicing into Travis.

"You must make yourself comfortable," Travis said with undisguised mockery as his eyes took in the empty liquor glasses. "I'm sure you'll both excuse us. Susan and I are tired after our flight and want to rest before dinner. We'll see the two of you then."

He steered Susan back across the verandah and into the house. When they were alone in a large bedroom containing a massive bed with a tall, carved mahogany headboard and several other articles of dark furniture, Susan said, "I had the impression you haven't seen your cousins in some time."

"It's been years."

"Is Violet Curt's sister? They have different last names."

"Yes. She was married the last I heard of her—may still be, but I doubt it. I can't see Violet being content as a homemaker."

"I don't mind if you want to go back down and talk to them," Susan said carefully. "It seems rude to leave them like that."

"It's rude to visit someone without giving some advance notice of your arrival," Travis returned.

The unexpected appearance of Curt and Violet had put him in a black mood and Susan realized that she was seeing a side of her husband's character that hadn't surfaced before. She didn't pursue the matter. Instead, she said, "I think I'll have a bath and lie down for a bit."

"Yes, that's a good idea. I have to look up my overseer and find out how the work is going here. Forgive me, please? Dinner will be at eight. I'll come back and change before that." He kissed her briefly and left.

She couldn't help feeling a little hurt at the abrupt change in his manner toward her, after all that talk on the plane about wanting to be alone with her. But she would have to get used to having his work claim much of his time and attention, and she supposed she might as well start now.

The bathroom adjoining the bedroom was a surprise; it had obviously been remodeled in recent years. A chocolate-brown shag carpet covered the floor, and the fixtures were soft yellow. The tub was the most impressive; it was at least twice the size of ordinary tubs and partially sunk below floor level so that one had to step down into it. There was also a separate stall shower in one corner.

As she bathed, Susan puzzled over her husband's strained relationship with his cousins and wondered why, given that, they should want to come for a visit. Perhaps Travis would explain later, when he was in a more amiable frame of mind. She finished her bath and returned to the bedroom to find that her luggage had been brought up.

She lay down across the white cotton bedspread in her slip. Almost immediately she was asleep and didn't awaken until seven-thirty when Travis came back to change for dinner. He was wearing a chambray shirt and jeans, and was damp with perspiration—and he still looked annoyed.

"Is anything wrong?" Susan asked, sitting up in the bed. "Anything else, I mean?"

He shook his head and began stripping off his shirt. "Not really. We've fallen behind with the cane, but that happens periodically."

"Did you get a chance to talk to Curt and Violet?"

He walked toward the bathroom. "I'll have all the conversation with them that I want at dinner."

Susan got up and put on a blue cotton tiered skirt and a cool white batiste peasant blouse with white sandals. Then she brushed her hair and secured it away from her face with combs at her temples. She hoped Travis's cousins didn't stay long, since their mere presence seemed to make him bristle.

Dinner was an uncomfortable affair, salvaged only by the delicious food Mala and Amii had prepared—tender, butter-basted flying fish, candied yams and a salad of fresh native fruits and melon balls. An excellent white wine was served with the meal, which was completed with raspberry ice and coffee.

The conversation between Travis and his cousins was stilted and punctuated with incomprehensible innuendos from Violet, who frequently looked at Susan in a way that seemed to be assessing. Just why she was being assessed,

Susan didn't know, nor did she care very much. She just wanted the meal to end and enough time to pass so that she could excuse herself without seeming inhospitable and go back upstairs.

It seemed forever before that could be accomplished. When at last she was in the bedroom again, she expected Travis to follow her shortly. But he didn't. She sat up for a long time, waiting for him. When he didn't come, she decided that he must have unbent enough to try to make up for his earlier rudeness with his cousins. They were probably talking more easily, now that the three of them were alone. She tried not to feel left out of her husband's life, but it was difficult.

She began to feel drowsy and changed into a sheer yellow gown. She turned out the light and opened louvered wooden doors to step out onto the private balcony. She leaned against the railing and listened to the sounds of night creatures—frogs and something that sounded like the crickets at home and occasionally the melancholy cry of a bird.

As she stood there, she heard male voices from below raised in anger. Travis and Curt had apparently left the house and were standing in a side courtyard, but she couldn't see them, nor could she make out their words. Only the anger was clear. Then the voices stopped and, shortly, she heard a car leaving, its tires crunching on the drive.

Still Travis did not come upstairs, and finally she couldn't stay awake any longer. She got into the bed, which seemed very large and lonely without Travis. In the darkness, she gave in to her hurt feelings at being neglected and let the tears come unchecked.

The last thought she had before sleep overtook her was that she had never expected to go to bed on her wedding night alone.

Shortly before dawn, Susan dreamed that she was in Travis's arms. She stirred and tried to burrow more deeply into the dream, not wanting it to end.

"Umm, you feel good." Travis's voice was a husky whisper in her ear.

She reached out to touch the solid hardness of his shoulder and realized that she wasn't dreaming. "Travis," she mumbled sleepily, "I've missed you. What have you been doing?"

"Thinking about you." He tugged at her gown. "I don't like nightgowns."

She let him pull the wispy fabric over her head and snuggled close to him. "I'll remember to wear pajamas after this," she teased.

He growled and nuzzled the tautened tip of one breast with his lips while he slid his hand over her stomach and hips, exploring, awakening her senses.

"I want you, Susan," he murmured, a ragged edge to the words.

Sensuous delight flowed through all her veins and she squirmed invitingly as he moved on top of her. A shudder ran down his long frame as they began to move together. The wild longing inside her built ever higher until at last it peaked and disintegrated, sending quivering sparks of pleasure through her.

Trembling, she sighed, "Oh, Travis, I love you."

He murmured her name and, rolling off her, wrapped his arms around her, clasping her to him.

Lazy and fulfilled, Susan pressed her cheek against his chest and drifted back into sleep.

When she awoke, sunlight was streaming across the bed from the balcony; she had failed to close the louvered doors completely the night before. She felt for Travis beside her, and did not find him. Then she saw him standing in the shadows beside the closet, tucking a work shirt into his jeans. She sat up, pulling the slipping sheet up to cover her nakedness.

"I guess the real world has overtaken us," she observed, wrinkling her nose at him. "You're going to take time for breakfast, aren't you, before you trudge out to the fields?"

He came to sit on the side of the bed to pull on tall leather boots. "Mala will have something waiting for me. I usually eat it on the run. You might as well go back to sleep for a while."

"Will I see you at lunch time?"

"I doubt it. I'll probably eat with the hands wherever they happen to be working at noon." He finished putting on his boots and bent to kiss her quickly, but thoroughly. He straightened and brushed the hair off her forehead, his touch gentle. "I don't think Curt and Violet will be around, either. You won't be too lonely, will you?"

"I'll find something to do. Can you leave me the car keys? I thought I might go into town."

"They're on the dresser. Remember to drive on the left side of the road."

She touched his cheek and smiled at him with

love in her eyes. "I'm sure the other drivers will remind me if I forget. Was that your car I heard driving away from the house last night?"

"Yes. I went to the bank."

"At that hour?"

"I wanted to take a look at the correspondence that had arrived in my absence and see if the manager had left any messages for me. You should have seen the pile of mail on my desk. It took me three hours to get through it."

"You warned me you worked long days, but you never said anything about the nights."

"It doesn't happen ordinarily," he assured her. "But I knew I'd be working on the plantation today and wanted to check in. Except for the mail backlog, they seem to have gotten along very well without me."

"Do you spend much time at the bank?"

He shook his head. "A few hours one or two days a week, except for board meetings and emergencies, which don't arise very often." He kissed the tip of her nose and got to his feet. "Want me to tell Mala to bring your breakfast up on a tray?"

"I'd rather go downstairs. I want to explore my new home."

He stood beside the bed, looking down at her for a long moment. There was something in his eyes that she didn't understand, and it made a tiny feeling of apprehension go through her. "I want you to be happy here, Susan."

"I'll be happy wherever you are."

His eyes cleared and he said, "I'll try to be home by six."

She watched him go, then got out of bed

and dressed quickly in khaki shorts and a cotton knit shirt with wide red and white stripes. Briefly she thought about unpacking before going downstairs, but decided to put it off until later. Maybe if she hurried, she would catch another look at Travis before he left the house.

Mala was in the kitchen alone, however. "'Mornin', Miz Susan," she said. "You like breakfast now?"

"Yes, please. I think I could eat a horse."

"I fix Mistah Travis eggs, bacon and biscuits every mornin'. What I fix you?"

"That sounds fine."

"You go on in the dining room then. I bring it in awhile."

Susan would have liked to stay and get better acquainted with the woman, but she sensed that she could not force Mala to accept her. She would have to prove that she would be good for Travis first. She also sensed that Mala might be resentful of intruders in her kitchen.

She wandered into the dining room and on through several other rooms—a large living room filled with Victorian furniture and a faded floral-patterned carpet, a smaller, sunnier sitting room with white wicker furniture that Susan found much more attractive and a masculine-looking paneled study with book-lined shelves and a desk.

When she returned to the dining room, Violet was sitting at one end of the long, linen-covered table. She looked very attractive in a lime-green sundress, her hair twisted atop her head in a loose bun.

"Good morning, Violet," Susan greeted her. "I didn't expect to see you. Travis thought you'd be away from the house today. Anyway, I'm glad I won't have to eat breakfast alone."

"You'd think Travis could have stayed around on your first day here," Violet remarked.

Susan refused to admit, even to herself, that the same thought had occurred to her. She took a chair near the other woman. "He warned me before we married that he works very hard. I'll have to find something to occupy my time, I guess."

"A job? I don't think Travis would care for that."

"I've no desire to pursue my former career. I was thinking more along the lines of volunteer work."

"That's wise, since you and Travis will be starting a family."

The odd note in Violet's statement perplexed Susan. "I hope we will. Both of us want children." Seeing what she thought was contempt on Violet's face, she quieted abruptly.

"What was the former career you mentioned?"

"I was a professional singer. That's how I met Travis. He came into the club in Miami where I was singing."

Violet's green eyes held an almost cunning look. She really was a curious woman, Susan decided, not the sort that she'd choose as a close friend. Mala appeared then with their breakfast and Violet continued to regard Susan keenly until Mala had served them and gone back to the kitchen.

Then she said, "When was that?"

Susan looked up from buttering a biscuit. "Sorry, you've lost me."

Violet was shaking a generous amount of salt over her scrambled eggs. "When was it that Travis came into the club where you were singing?"

Susan recalled that Travis had declined to answer a similar question from Curt the night before. But his attitude toward his cousins would probably cause him to consider any question from them impertinent. She saw no reason to hide the fact that she and Travis had known each other such a short time. People might raise eyebrows, but in time they would realize that they had known what they were doing.

"About a week ago," she said in a matter-of-fact tone.

Violet's green eyes flew up to Susan's face. "My God!"

Susan laughed at her stunned expression. "Why, Violet, I do believe I've shocked you."

Her eyes narrowed. "You don't strike me as being gullible where men are concerned."

Her choice of words surprised Susan. She wondered suddenly if Violet was baiting her. She took a bite of her egg before she responded. "I don't think I am, but I'm not bitter on the subject, either. I get the feeling that you are. Aren't you married?"

"Divorced," Violet said shortly.

"Not amicably, I gather."

"It was dreadful. Not just the divorce, but the marriage as well." She uttered a brittle little laugh. "My hormones overcame my common

94

sense or I'd never have agreed to marry him in the first place. I already knew that men are beasts and marriage merely confirmed me in that opinion." She looked steadily into Susan's eyes. "I've never met a man who can be trusted."

"I've known a few like that, too," Susan said, "but you can't paint them all with the same brush. We don't like it when they apply sweeping generalizations to women."

Violet shrugged. "I can understand why you'd want to rationalize your reasons for marrying Travis, but if you say that he swept you off your feet, I'll scream."

Susan smiled slightly as she helped herself to pineapple preserves. She didn't think Violet was thirty yet, but it certainly hadn't taken long for her to become a died-in-the-wool cynic. She felt rather sorry for the woman, and she was coming to understand why Travis didn't like having her around.

"I won't use that old cliché then," she said, "but truthfully, that's very nearly what happened." She saw Violet's disbelieving stare and went on, "I'm not a naive teenager, Violet, and I'd given up believing in love at first sight years ago—until I met Travis."

Violet was very still all at once. "Dear me," she murmured finally, "this is even worse than I thought."

Susan frowned. "Worse? How?"

Susan stared at her and then she began to detect some of what was behind the other woman's words. "I suppose you assumed I married him for his money." She found that she resented the fact that Violet had jumped to her own cynical conclusions and hastened to set her straight. "I had an idea that Travis was prosperous, but I didn't realize how much so. I wouldn't have cared if he'd been destitute, though. We married because we love each other, and that's the only reason."

Violet's green eyes glittered. "You can't blame me for being skeptical—under the circumstances."

Susan's irritation was growing. "I don't know what you're hinting at, but I'd prefer that you speak plainly. It's obvious that you don't approve of the fact that Travis is married. Is it jealousy?"

"Jealousy!" The redhead croaked out the word. "Oh, my dear Susan, you *are* naive, no matter what you say." She drained her coffee cup, all the while gazing at Susan over the rim. As she set it down, she added, "Well, enjoy it while you can. You'll discover what you've gotten yourself into soon enough."

Susan was rigid. "Would you care to explain what you mean by that?"

She seemed to be deliberating with herself before she said, "No, I don't want to be the one to tell you." She fingered her cutlery. "I will give you one piece of advice, though. Whenever you have a chance, ask Anthony Valdez about the will."

"Anthony Valdez? I've never heard of him."

"He's Travis's attorney."

Susan pushed back her chair. "Apparently you get some kind of kick out of talking in circles. I don't enjoy it myself. If you'll excuse me, I have things to do."

At that moment, Curt strode into the room, smoke curling from the end of the cigarette protruding from the ivory holder clamped in his mouth. He looked agitated. Without greeting either of the women, he said to Violet, "After six phone calls, I finally found two available hotel rooms. How soon can you be ready to go?"

"Thirty minutes," Violet said.

Susan looked from one to the other. "You're going to a hotel?"

"Oh, didn't Travis tell you?" Curt inquired peevishly. "He invited us to leave."

Susan could think of no appropriate reply to that, so she murmured, "Well, if I don't see you before you go, good-bye." She couldn't bring herself to utter the hypocritical claim that she was pleased to have met them. After her conversation with Violet, she wanted them out of the house as much as Travis did.

Curt and Violet exchanged a speaking look. Wondering about the strange behavior of the two, Susan left the room to go upstairs. By the time she reached the bedroom, she realized that she was actually a little disturbed by Violet's enigmatic remarks at breakfast. She suspected that the woman had been trying to make her question the wisdom of having married Travis so quickly. Did Violet really believe that she, a total stranger, could come between Susan and the man she loved so deeply—and while they were still honeymooners, too? It was so ludicrous that Susan laughed aloud.

As for Curt, he had looked angry enough to explode just now at having to go to a hotel. Surely he hadn't thought that Travis would welcome them into his home, for it was evident that there was animosity of long standing between her husband and his cousins. At least Curt had cleared up one thing for her. Last night, when she had heard the men's angry voices in the courtyard, they had evidently been arguing over Curt's and Violet's moving out. Though why Curt would even bother to argue, she didn't know; this was Travis's house and he didn't want them here.

Her husband's cousins were definitely strange, she told herself. And she wasn't going to spend anymore time trying to figure them out. Whatever there was between Travis and them had nothing to do with her, although she suspected, from Violet's mention of the attorney, that she and her brother might resent the division Travis's grandfather had made of his estate. Had they wanted the plantation instead of the stocks and bonds that Travis said had been left to them? Susan shook her head and rid herself of the question. Probably the less she knew about it the better for all concerned. There was nothing worse than family squabbling after someone had died.

Her glance fell on her suitcases, and she decided to unpack and give Curt and Violet time enough to leave before she ventured downstairs again. The room's large closet was practically empty. Travis must keep his clothing in another room. Perhaps he hadn't used this bedroom before his marriage.

She took her time removing things from her suitcases and hanging them in an ordered fashion in the closet—first dresses, then blouses and shirts and finally skirts and pants. Then she set her shoes in a row on the floor beneath the clothes.

The large chest of drawers was empty, too, so she arranged her nightgowns and underthings in it. Then she carried her cosmetic bag into the bathroom and set everything on a tier of glass shelves on the wall next to a large mirror with a wide gilt frame.

When she was sure she had given Curt and Violet plenty of time to be gone, she spent the next hour exploring the house. There were even more rooms than she had expected, and all of generous proportions.

The second floor contained six bedrooms and four baths. She counted eight rooms downstairs. In addition to the living and dining room, sitting room, kitchen and study that she'd already seen, there was a room containing a small organ and a grand piano, another more formal parlor, and a large pantry next to the kitchen, where nonperishable foodstuffs were stored. When she questioned Mala she learned that the laundry was done in a separate wash house behind the garages in back and that Mala and Amii lived with their husbands in another house still farther back.

As Travis had said, the furniture was old, but some of it looked to be of very good quality. Although the carpets and window coverings in some of the rooms were rather worn, there was a general atmosphere of old-fashioned gentility throughout the house. Of course, Susan could see many ways in which the decor could be made to look more cheerful. Travis had said that she could do some redecorating as they could afford it, indicating that, in spite of his assets, he might not be rolling in ready cash. But it didn't matter. She liked the house as it was and could be patient about changing things. For now it was enough to live there with Travis.

Her exploration complete, she went back upstairs for the car keys and her purse, stopping in the kitchen on her way out to tell Mala that she wouldn't want any lunch after the hearty breakfast she'd had. If she felt hungry later, she'd get something in town.

She drove into Bridgetown in the sports car, giving her undivided attention to staying on the left side of the road and wondering how long it would be before that became second nature to her. Not long, she hoped, for she wanted to explore the entire island in the coming days.

The capital was bustling with traffic that crawled along the narrow streets and throngs of pedestrians on the sidewalks. From the fresh sunburns and vacation clothing they wore, Susan guessed that a good percentage of the shoppers were tourists. She found a parking space near Lord Nelson's statue and dashed across the street to meander along the main thoroughfare, window shopping and occasionally going into an establishment that looked interesting.

She spent a half hour in a bookstore where she finally bought a volume on the history of Barbados and another dealing strictly with Bridgetown. She wanted to learn all she could about the island.

Just after noon, she stopped in a drugstore for

iced tea, looking through one of the books she'd purchased while she drank it and rested a bit.

She smiled as she read the author's statement that the first institution the English always established in a new colony was a drinking house, in contrast to the Spaniards, who always began with a church building and the Dutch, who always started by erecting a fort. However, Bridgetown's British settlers had built a church, St. Michael's, in 1630, and now there was a newer church on the same site called St. Mary's. Since it was only two blocks from where she sat, she decided to have a look at it.

The church was large and built of gray stone. There was some construction in progress, perhaps merely restoration work, so Susan decided not to go inside. She wandered about the old churchyard for a while, trying to make out the faded carving on the markers.

Finally she headed back along Broad Street toward where she had left the car. About halfway to her destination, the scroll lettering on a sign hanging over one of the shops caught her eye: "Kay's Boutique." Deciding that it had to be the shop operated by Travis's friend, Kay Harte, she went inside.

At the back, a petite black-haired woman, wearing a cool, white shirtwaist dress, was waiting on a customer. Susan browsed through a rack of dresses until the customer had paid for her purchases and left. As she walked over to the counter, the black-haired woman looked up and smiled. She wasn't pretty, but she had an open, pleasant face and was meticulously groomed with every smooth black hair in place.

"Hello. May I help you?"

"I'm looking for Kay Harte."

"You've found her." She was still smiling at Susan expectantly.

Susan extended her hand. "I'm Susan Sennett, Travis's wife."

Although she knew there hadn't been time for word to get around about Travis's marriage, she wasn't quite prepared for Kay Harte's extreme reaction. The blood left her face in a rush and her brown eyes seemed about to pop from her head for a moment. When she recovered she shook hands, her fingers clammy and cold.

"Forgive me, but you've really shocked me."

Susan laughed. "I can see that."

"It's a pleasure to meet you, Susan."

"Thank you. Travis mentioned that he particularly wanted me to get to know you. I hope we'll be close friends."

There was a pained look in Kay Harte's eyes as she said, "So do I." It came to Susan in a flash that the woman was in love with Travis.

"I'm not having many customers today," Kay was saying. "Let me make us a cup of tea."

"That would be very nice." Susan followed her to a small office in the back and took a chair while Kay put a pot of water on a hotplate and readied tea bags in two cups. After she had made the tea and handed Susan hers, she sat down behind the desk.

"Where are you from?"

"I was living in Miami until yesterday."

"I knew that Travis had gone to Miami to consult his lawyer, but obviously the trip wasn't strictly for business." She set her cup down and shook her head. "I don't mean to be rude, but I'm still a little stunned by this. How long have you known Travis?"

Everybody she met here seemed to ask that question, Susan thought. For some reason, she wanted to evade a direct answer with Kay Harte. "Not extremely long. You know how it is. Sometimes you meet that rare individual and, in a short period of time, you feel as though you know him as well as you know yourself. Perhaps it has to do with wave lengths."

"Uh-huh," Kay murmured, "I suppose."

"Anyway, I've never been so happy in my life, and I'm sure I'm going to love Barbados." Then she added seriously, "I know that you and Travis have always been close friends. I want you to know that I'm going to be a good wife to him. He's happy, and I intend to keep him that way."

"As Travis's friend, I only want what's best for him. I'm glad that he's happy. Aside from having acquired a very lovely wife, he must have had hopeful news from his attorney about having his grandfather's will declared invalid."

Susan's lashes came down to veil the fact that Kay's remark had left her completely at sea. "Yes," she murmured. "I don't think there was anything definite, but you know how legal matters drag on forever."

Kay was watching her intently. Then they heard the faint sound of a bell tinkling and she made a face. "I have a customer. Excuse me, please."

Susan set her tea aside and got to her feet. "I won't take up any more of your time. I just wanted to stop and say hello."

"I'm awfully glad you did. I hope we'll be seeing each other again soon."

Susan mumbled an agreement, followed the other woman out of the office, said good-bye and left the shop. She walked toward the car, her curiosity awakened. Both Kay and Violet had mentioned that will. She had thought that Travis was well satisfied with inheriting the plantation and his grandfather's interest in the bank. But if he had seen his lawyer about breaking the will, he apparently wasn't. Maybe that's what he and Curt had disagreed over last night, instead of whether Curt and Violet would move to a hotel, as she had assumed.

Chapter Six

Susan dressed for dinner with care that evening. It would be the first meal she and Travis had shared alone since their arrival, and she had asked Mala to set up a table on the back veranda. She was wearing a deep-aqua silk dress with a halter top, bared back and full skirt. A silver necklace with a turquoise drop and small turquoise earrings complemented the dress perfectly. Her hair fell in loose waves about her face without combs or fasteners to impede it, because Travis liked it that way.

Travis came out of the bathroom wearing a terry robe. She had hardly seen him when he came in from the fields and headed straight for the shower and, at the sight of his still damp, tousled hair and the glowing bronze of his skin, her heart seemed to turn over.

He stood still and looked at her. "Hello, wife." His eyes devoured her as if he couldn't get enough, and she felt warmth rush through every part of her body. "Come here," he said very softly.

"Nothing doing," she breathed. "As certain as

I do, we'll be late for dinner. We're having it on the veranda and I—I think I'd better go down and see how Mala is coming along."

"Hard-hearted woman," he growled as she slipped past him and out the door.

She found both Mala and Amii in the kitchen. "Is there anything I can do to help?"

Amii, who was stirring something in a pot on the stove, turned to look at her and giggle. "You're very pretty, Miss Susan."

"Thank you, Amii."

Mala's hands moved deftly over a cutting board. "You stay here, you get that nice frock stained. You go out and see how you like the table I fix for you. We makin' a fine feast."

Susan obeyed. The table sat next to the wrought-iron railing, out of reach of the light coming through the kitchen windows. But the full moon provided enough light to illuminate an arrangement of pale wild orchids in the center of a white cloth. Silver glowed with a soft patina in the moonlight. Susan sighed happily and turned as Mala appeared with a silver tray, which she set on one of the small patio tables.

"This special recipe," she told Susan. "Poached oyster canapes with caviar to go with cocktails. You try."

Susan lifted one of the crisp toast rounds in the center of which sat an oyster ringed with caviar and sour cream. She nibbled tentatively, then finished the canape with a groan of approval. "Mala, these are delicious! You've outdone yourself."

"You like everything else, too." Her tone was clearly pleased. "I tell Mistah Travis bring your drink when he come out." With a rustle of cotton skirts, she returned to the kitchen.

Moments later, Travis appeared, dressed in dark trousers and an open-collared shirt. He carried two stemmed glasses. "I brought white wine for you. Is that all right?"

"Perfect," Susan told him, accepting the drink and standing on tiptoe to kiss him lightly. "Come and try Mala's wonderful canapes. I told her this was a special occasion, and she's really pulling out all the stops."

"In a minute." He reached for her with his free hand and pulled her against him. "After I have a proper kiss," which he proceeded to claim. As always when he held her, a lovely warmth uncurled inside her and she relaxed against him, her breasts crushed against his chest.

When he released her, she sighed reluctantly but took his hand and led him to two patio chairs near the canape tray. When they were seated, she sipped her wine and said, "I guess you know that Curt and Violet moved to a hotel this morning."

"Yes. I told them we were on our honeymoon and suggested it would be considerate of them to make themselves scarce."

"I had breakfast with Violet before they left. Honestly, Travis, I don't understand that woman. Some of the things she said made no sense at all."

She was aware of a tenseness in him. "Such as?"

"Well—for one thing, when I said that I loved you, she seemed to think it highly improbable.

I'm sure she believes I married you for your money."

He made a sarcastic sound. "Voilet would. She thinks every woman is as mercenary as she is. I feel sorry for that poor fool she married."

"She told me they're divorced. She also said she doesn't trust men."

He laughed shortly. "Mr. Graves is well out of it."

"There was something else, Travis," Susan said thoughtfully. "I got the distinct impression that she and Curt aren't happy with the way your grandfather's estate was divided. She didn't say it in so many words, but I had the feeling that they wanted the plantation. Isn't that odd? They don't strike me as people who would be content here, so far away from a really cosmopolitan city, like London."

"They wouldn't be," Travis retorted. "If they want the plantation, it's only for the price it would bring on a sale."

"But didn't you say your grandfather left them a valuable stock portfolio?"

"Yes, but the bank and plantation made up well over half the value of the estate. Harris left them to me because I came home two years ago to manage them for him. More to the point, he knew I'd continue to operate the plantation after he was gone, keep it in the family. That was important to him. But Curt and Violet feel they were cheated."

"I didn't realize . . ." The unequal division of the estate accounted for at least some of the animosity between Travis and his cousins.

"Is that why they're here? Do they want you to hand over part of your share?"

"They'd like nothing better. I give them three years at the outside to run through those stocks and bonds, and I've no intention of providing them with another penny. Susan, if either of them comes around here again, I don't want you to talk to them. They're troublemakers."

"I don't really want to see them. They make me feel . . . uncomfortable."

Mala and Amii began to serve the meal, and they moved to the table. The main course was a smoked salmon quiche served with crisp vegetables and wine.

"Tell me something, Mala," Travis teased as he spread his napkin. "Why is it I have to get married before you'll make my favorite quiche? We haven't had this in years."

"I los' recipe," Mala said with a mischievous grin that made her teeth flash white in the moonlight. "Besides, mon, why I waste fancy meals on you? You jes eat standin' up, then rush off without dessert. Sometimes you not eat at all."

Travis reached across the table and clasped Susan's hand. "Things will be different now."

"'Bout time, too," Mala retorted as she turned to leave the veranda.

"I think she's beginning to like me a little," Susan confided.

Travis chuckled. "How could she help it? That doesn't mean she won't boss you around, just as she does me. The woman's a tartar, but don't let it upset you."

"Don't worry. My feelings aren't easily hurt."

He looked up from his plate, his eyes meeting hers with an odd, fleeting expression. But when he spoke, it was to say something complimentary about the food. They ate in silence for several moments and Susan thought back over what Travis had told her about his grandfather's will and the reason for his cousins' obvious displeasure. And suddenly she remembered her stop at the boutique that afternoon.

"I almost forgot to tell you," she said. "I met your friend Kay Harte today. I was in town and happened onto her shop, so I introduced myself. After she recovered from the shock, she gave me a cup of tea."

Travis smiled. "Maybe we should send out a few announcements to pave the way for you before you meet any more of my friends. We don't want anyone having a stroke."

"Announcements sound like a good idea."

"So, did you like Kay?"

"Very much. She's extremely fond of you."

"As I am of her."

But not in the same way, Susan thought, seeing again the wounded look that had been in Kay's eyes for a moment when Susan had said that she was Travis's wife. She also remembered Kay mentioning that Travis went to Miami to have his grandfather's will declared invalid. She wondered now if perhaps Kay had misunderstood Travis's reason for going. He'd gotten the plantation that he loved, and the bank— more than half of the estate. Why should he want to change that?

"Darling, Kay said something that puzzled me."

"Oh?" There was that sudden alertness again.

"She said that you went to Miami to see your lawyer about having your grandfather's will set aside."

He did not answer immediately, and for some reason Susan began to wish that she had kept Kay's remark to herself. Finally she realized that he was angry when she saw his hand clenching his fork. "I wish," he said in a stiff voice, "that people would not discuss my personal affairs on the main street of Bridgetown."

Dismayed, she said, "But it wasn't like that at all. Kay wasn't gossiping. She only mentioned it in passing. I didn't say that you had told me nothing about it, although I confess it made me feel a little shut out. Why didn't you mention it to me, Travis?"

He looked at her for a moment. "The fewer people who know about something so delicate and iffy, the better," he said finally. "For one thing, I don't want Curt and Violet to get wind of it."

"Then it's true?"

After another moment, he said, "Yes."

"But why do you want to change the will? It seems to me you should be happy the way things are." Surely he hadn't expected to get *everything*?

He drew a long breath and glanced at his hand clasping his fork. The fingers relaxed. "I am—basically. Only the will puts some . . . restrictions on what can be done with the land that could make things . . . difficult. I don't want to sell an acre, but if, for example, we had a total crop failure, it might be necessary. I just don't like having my hands tied, even loosely."

He spoke slowly, as if he were picking each word with great care. Why did she have the feeling he wasn't being completely candid with her? "What did the lawyer say? Can the will be broken?"

"No. I'll have to live with things as they are." She said on a lighter note, "*I'm* grateful to your grandfather for putting those restrictions in the will."

"Why?"

"Because they made you come to Miami and find me."

He smiled ruefully. "I didn't mean to snap at you just now."

"Did I ever tell you," she went on, "that you made me very uncomfortable those first two nights in the Top Hat, sitting there and staring at me all the way through my act?"

"I was imagining how you would look in my bed."

Susan uttered a soft laugh. "I didn't do that with you until the first time you kissed me. Now I do it all the time."

His eyes narrowed provocatively. "You don't really want dessert, do you?"

"Mala will kill us if we don't sample everything. You really must learn to be patient."

"Mala," he called and when she appeared in the kitchen doorway he told her that they were ready for dessert.

Susan relaxed and let her mind veer from the

confusing conversation about the will. A small nagging voice in her brain suggested that she felt totally secure and at ease with Travis only when they were making love—or talking about it. But she reminded herself that she would come to understand all the varied aspects of his character in time. And they had plenty of that.

Thinking of what was to come when they were once more in the privacy of their bedroom, Susan managed to eat only a few bites of the spiced apple cake topped with whipped cream. She gave no more thought to Travis's seeming overreaction to what Kay Harte had said. When Mala came out to see if they wanted anything else, Susan said, "I was too full before the cake came, Mala. Maybe you could put mine in the refrigerator until tomorrow."

She and Travis walked up the stairs hand in hand. In their bedroom, his arms tightened around her and the yielding weakness swept over her again. His kiss was hard and demanding at first, and then his mouth softened to coax and seduce. His hands slid down her body and sent excitement tingling to her brain. He fumbled with the halter's closing at the back of her neck, finally freeing it and pushing the fabric down and away from her. His hands slid silkily over her warm, smooth skin, cupping and lifting her breasts.

Her fingers stroked his thick hair and followed the strong line of his shoulders. She murmured, "Love me, Travis," the words muffled by the drugging intoxication of his mouth against her own.

Then he lifted her and laid her on the bed

where he disposed of the remainder of her clothing and his own. He stretched beside her and she met his descending mouth urgently, her hands tracing paths over his back and shoulders as the restlessness of her sensual need grew.

"My beautiful, beautiful Susan," he whispered hoarsely. His hands and lips caressed her body, eliciting soft little moans of pleasure. Finally their lovemaking grew fierce and she felt passion rising in her like a tidal wave, drowning all else as she climbed with him toward the ultimate fulfillment.

She slept deeply, and when she awoke next morning Travis had already left the house. She lay in bed, gazing out a window over cane fields and beyond to the green-black ridges of sprawling hills, their outlines blurred by mist. The lowering sky was grayish-white and, as she lay there, her thoughts drifting aimlessly over ways in which she might occupy her day, rain began to patter softly on the roof. She dressed, resigning herself to being confined to the house all day by the weather.

At breakfast, she asked Mala, "Do you have weekends off?"

Mala shrugged indifferently. "Sometimes, if Mistah Travis not need us here. I try to cook enough food on Friday to last him till Monday—things that he can eat cold or warm up in the oven without any bother."

"From now on you won't have to worry about that," Susan told her. "I'll cook for us on the weekends."

The woman looked doubtful. "If you sure it's not too much trouble."

"Mala, I'll enjoy it. I'm used to working, and I can't spend my days doing nothing."

"If you say so, Miz Susan. Amii and me, we like having our weekends at home."

"Good. Then that's settled."

After breakfast, Susan wandered restlessly through the house, ending up in Travis's study; its masculine aura made him seem close to her. The room smelled of old leather, wax and Travis's cheroots. She scanned the bookshelves until she happened upon a novel she had been meaning to read. She settled into a comfortable leather armchair, book in hand.

The author was one of her favorites, but she couldn't lose herself in his crisp, honed language as she usually did. Her thoughts kept wandering to the baffling tenseness—almost a wariness— she had sensed in Travis since they'd returned to the island. She was certain it had something to do with his grandfather's will and Travis's, as well as his cousins', dissatisfaction with it. Why had Travis been so elusive when she'd asked him about the will last night at dinner? Now that she thought back over what he had said, she realized that he had actually given her no specific information at all. Yet Kay Harte seemed to be in his confidence, and Susan couldn't help feeling hurt by that. He and Kay had been friends for years, but now *she* was his wife. How were they to build this marriage into a strong, secure relationship if he wouldn't be totally open and honest with her?

She recalled her last conversation with Violet. "You'll discover soon enough what you've gotten yourself into," the woman had said. What on earth had she meant by that? Susan suspected that it was like Violet to hint broadly at something outrageous and then refuse to elaborate, just as she had done when Susan asked her to explain her remark. Violet had fallen back on that old excuse, "I don't want to be the one to tell you," although it was clear that she had been dying to. Why hadn't she? Had Travis warned her not to, that first evening when Susan had gone up to bed alone and left him downstairs with his cousins?

The thought made her uncomfortable, but it was one possible explanation for Violet's uncharacteristic reticence. She had suggested that Susan speak to Travis's lawyer. It was as if Violet really wanted her to know some family secret, but was afraid to tell Susan herself. Afraid of what Travis would do?

Susan's glance fell on the telephone on Travis's desk. Did she dare call the lawyer, Anthony Valdez, in Miami? What reason could she give him for wanting to know about Harris Sennett's will? And how would Travis react if Valdez told him that she had called? A chill of apprehension went through her. It was a crazy idea, and yet she couldn't get it out of her mind. Again and again, her glance drifted to the silent telephone, until it began to seem sentient, almost daring her to make the call.

She got up and paced about the room, a new wave of doubts assailing her. There was something in the will that Travis didn't want her to know, or he would have been more candid last night—something that Curt and Violet knew, something that Kay Harte knew. Why wouldn't Travis tell his wife? She didn't like the stirring of possibilities that began to surface in her mind. Travis didn't trust her with information concerning his private affairs as much as he trusted his old friend, Kay. Violet had hinted that it had something to do with Susan's reason for marrying Travis. Was Travis's marriage somehow tied in with the "restrictions" he had mentioned?

Her thoughts were becoming bewildering —and frightening. She suspected that she wouldn't feel reassured until she knew the will's provisions. If Travis's marriage was somehow endangering his inheritance, she had a right to know. She was an adult; she didn't need to be protected from unpleasantness by her husband.

Slowly she approached the desk. She touched the black telephone receiver, running her fingers along the smooth surface. Finally she lifted it, only then realizing that she had no idea how to get the information operator. She let out a long breath and dialed "O." An operator came on the line, and she asked for Florida information. After a series of clicks and pauses, another operator came on, and she requested Anthony Valdez's office number. It was all very simple, she thought, as she jotted down the number on a pad beside the telephone.

Before her wavering resolve could desert her completely, she dialed. Valdez's secretary informed her that he was "busy." She almost gave up then, but she disliked the woman's impatient tone.

"Tell him it's Mrs. Travis Sennett," Susan said with authority. "I'm sure he'll talk to me."

After a few moments a male voice said, "Mrs. Sennett? This is Tony Valdez."

Suddenly Susan felt foolish and even a little panicky. What did she say now? "Er—how are you, Mr. Valdez?"

"Fine. I had a wire from Travis informing me of your marriage. Allow me to congratulate you."

"Thank you." She sensed a guardedness in the voice and knew that she would learn nothing from Anthony Valdez that he thought Travis didn't want her to know.

"What can I do for you, Mrs. Sennett?"

The moment of truth had come and Susan decided that, since she had dared this much, she might as well fling all caution to the wind. Travis was certain to learn of this call eventually, anyway. "I'm calling about Harris Sennett's will, Mr. Valdez. I—I know you are in Travis's confidence and—" She wasn't sure where she was going, what would loosen Valdez's tongue, but she plunged on. "Well, you know the . . . problems connected with our marriage—at this time." Dear heaven, she wasn't making the slightest sense. Valdez probably thought she was hysterical—or insane.

But amazingly, she seemed to have said the right words. When Valdez responded, he sounded less guarded. "I'm glad Travis confided in you. Obviously, you're a special sort of woman. Old Mr. Sennett's will might have hurried things along, but I'm sure Travis would have married you soon enough, regardless. I've never thought him a true bachelor at heart."

It was clear that the attorney assumed that she and Travis had known each other for some time, perhaps had been discussing marriage prior to Harris Sennett's death. Susan responded carefully, "I couldn't agree with you more. And it's not as if either of us is a child. We were both ready for marriage. The only fly in our ointment at the moment is Travis's cousins. They were here at the plantation before we arrived from Miami. They—they're making unreasonable requests, I'm afraid, and Travis is terribly concerned."

"I would advise both of you to ignore them."

"They've moved to a hotel, at Travis's request, but—"

"Mrs. Sennett, as I told Travis, his grandfather's will cannot be broken, if that's what his cousins have in mind. All Travis has to do is have a legitimate heir by the time he's thirty-five, and his cousins can't touch the plantation or the bank. Tell him to stop worrying. You might tell him, also, that I've been doing a little research and there are several precedents to indicate that a pregnancy within a legal marriage is all that is required. What I mean is that the child doesn't have to be born by Travis's thirty-fifth birthday, as long as it's on the way. Several legal decisions have recognized unborn children as persons with rights and privileges

under the law. That should make him feel less
. . . er, pressured."

As he spoke, a coldness crept over Susan. Now
she could hardly speak, because the muscles of
her throat felt as if they were frozen. Finally she
got out, "I'll tell him. Thank you, Mr. Valdez."

She lowered herself into a chair after the
telephone call. She felt shaken, but what Valdez
had told her did not, at first, come totally clear in
her mind. In those first moments she only knew
that she felt undone and that there was a trembling in her. Travis. She could see him as clearly
as if he stood in the room with her. A tall, rugged
man, strong and solid, yet capable of tenderness
—what was known as a man strong enough to be
gentle. "Travis," she whispered in the ominous
silence of the study.

She was to realize later that, in those first few
moments, she had been suffering from shock,
the body's instinctive defense against a pain
that is too terrible to be borne. But then the pain
came, huge, and causing a shrinking sensation
in her chest. She knew what had to be known,
and the coldness in her grew vast. When she
stood her legs were so weak that she almost fell.
She stumbled to the concealed bar, poured whiskey into a glass with a shaking hand and gulped
it. It set off a spasm of coughing and choking,
but eventually she got her breath.

Travis had married her because he had to
have an heir or lose the only thing in the world
that he held dear. She hadn't waited to hear all
the details of the will, but she had heard enough
to know that, without an heir, Curt and Violet

would come into part or all of Travis's inheritance. She had thought she was too experienced and worldly wise to be totally disillusioned by any man. Now she knew what terrible disillusionment was, numbing, crushing, making her shudder, turning her body to stone.

Then the whiskey hit her like a molten rock in the pit of her stomach, and she heard the sound of her own ponderous breathing. Everywhere she looked, things shimmered and wavered before her, as if the rain were inside the house with her, not merely sloshing mournfully against the window panes.

Now she understood what was behind all of Violet's innuendos, why everyone had asked how long she and Travis had known each other, why Travis had been so upset at seeing Curt and Violet, so angry because Kay had told her his reason for going to Miami. Now she understood why he had asked her to marry him after knowing her only a few days. He would have married almost anyone! Kay Harte had probably been his first choice, but she knew about the will and her pride probably wouldn't permit her to marry him under those circumstances, even though she was in love with him.

Everything was so dreadfully clear—now. She felt anguish spreading through her and closed her eyes for a moment. Then the tears started, hot, and racking her body. The sound was shattering in the heavy silence of the study with the melancholy murmur of rain in the background. Finally she became quieter, drawing great gulps of air.

The study door burst open and Travis stood framed in the opening, his clothing wet and pasted to him, his hair dripping. "I heard something—" He halted to stare at her white, still face. "You've been crying. Susan, what's happened?"

"What—are you doing here?" He could hardly hear her.

"I got caught in the rain. I came back to change and I heard you crying." He walked toward her slowly, but he didn't touch her. Somehow he sensed that that would be the worst thing he could do. "What's wrong?"

"You—" Her mouth was working and she had trouble getting the words out. "I'll never forgive you for this, Travis. Never!"

A rigid stillness settled on him. He knew. "What has Violet said to you?"

"I haven't seen Violet. I've just spoken to Anthony Valdez in Miami." She paused, hugging herself and rocking slightly. "How could I have been such a fool? I was so careful to be honest with you, telling you that I'd lost my job. I didn't want to keep anything from you and all the time—"

"Susan, listen to me. I know I should have told you. I would have—"

"When?" Her voice rose shrilly. "After our first child was born? On our tenth anniversary? On my deathbed? When, Travis—when—?"

His face twisted painfully. "Soon. I swear it. You must believe me."

"Believe you!" She began to laugh, and she couldn't stop.

Travis was shaking her. "Stop it, Susan!" The hideous sounds died in her throat and she stared up at him, her eyes great wounds in her white face.

He swallowed visibly. "We'll talk about this later when you're calmer—when you've come to your senses."

"I haven't been in command of my senses since the day I met you," she said with agonized bitterness. "Until now." How had he deceived her so utterly? She could hear the rain splattering with greater force against the windows, the sound of Travis's rasping breath, and the dull thudding of her own heart in her ears. Outside the sky darkened.

"I'm leaving you, Travis. You'll hear from my lawyer about the divorce."

That was when she saw something in him that she had never seen before. Inexorability. And yet, hadn't she sensed from the beginning his potential for ruthlessness?

"I won't let you go," he said. "I know everyone on this island. I'll distribute photographs. I'll leave word at the airport and harbors—everywhere—that I am to be called should you try to leave. We're married, Susan, and we're going to stay married."

She looked into his face and saw that he meant every word. A deadly calm settled over her. "All right, Travis. You give me no choice. You can make me stay, but you can't make me have your detestable heir. If you ever touch me again I—I'll try to kill you." She fought down another rising of hysteria. "I mean it. I hate you!

I can't stand the thought of you touching me now."

For a moment he stared at her, his jaw clamped. Then he turned and slammed out of the room. She lowered herself into a chair and began to weep again, involuntarily, silently. But there was no comfort in weeping.

Chapter Seven

Later, when she knew that Travis was gone, she went upstairs and found her hooded rain-coat.

She walked away from the house. The lawn and countryside beyond looked different through the rain—dark and torpid. Wet gravel crunched beneath her leather soles as she gained the drive and walked along it to the road. Her face was set. She was finished with crying. Nothing had changed in her situation; she had merely learned its true dimensions. It had never been a real marriage, with love and commitment, except in her deluded imagination.

I'll have to live with things as they are. Travis's words came back to her and she saw the meaning in them finally. Now he was going to force her to exist in the same wretchedness, although she doubted if he had yet perceived the depth of her loathing for him and what he had done. In time, he would. Maybe, after a few days when the pain was not so new, she would be able to look upon this as a holiday, a chance to come to know another culture, a chance to think about her life and where she wanted it to go from here.

125

When Travis saw that she really meant what she had said to him in the study, he would let her go and she could begin to put everything into perspective, see this as a time in her life when she had been a little demented and out of touch with reality. Surely, after enough time passed, she could forget. She was strong, and she would become stronger.

She walked for two hours, forcing down her pain and humiliation and replacing them with an iron resolve. By the time she returned to the house, she was wet through the thin plastic coat and weary beyond imagining. She brushed aside Mala's concern over her bedraggled state and went upstairs to bathe and lie down.

She slept until midafternoon and awoke with a scratchy throat and stuffy nose. She found aspirin in the bathroom and swallowed two tablets, then went downstairs. Mala served her a hot, hearty stew with cheese and crackers, and Susan found that, despite the unhappiness and a fuzzyheaded feeling, she could still eat. In fact, she finished off two filling bowls and complimented Mala on the lunch.

The older woman had been hovering near the dining room doorway ever since Susan had come downstairs. Now she ventured into the room. "You taking a cold, Miz Susan. You shouldn't stay out in the rain for so long."

"I needed to walk. Don't worry. No one ever died of a head cold."

"You seem different," Mala observed, her black eyes canny and inquisitive. "Is somethin' wrong?"

Evidently the maids had not heard that confrontation in the study and were unaware of her humiliation. She was grateful. She returned the other woman's look without blinking. "What could be wrong, Mala?"

Mala shrugged her thin shoulders. "Don't know. Somethin' different, though."

"Well, you know what they say." Susan's voice was brittle. "We wake up in a new world every morning." She didn't like herself much when she was being sarcastic, especially when the recipient was innocent of the cause. She forced her lips to curve in the semblance of a smile. "I think I'll take a big mug of hot tea upstairs with me. I probably won't want any dinner after such a late lunch. You'll convey my regrets to Travis, won't you?"

"Yes'm." Mala was looking as if she thought Susan might be suffering from delirium. "If you say so. You got the right idea. I fix your tea, and you rest."

Susan spent the afternoon in bed with a box of tissues at her elbow, reading the history of Barbados. Surprisingly, with her life in a shambles around her, she actually understood and remembered much of what she read, which only showed what a marvelous instrument the human brain is.

Travis knocked at the door at eight. "Susan, I want to talk to you."

She closed her book and lay back against the pillows. "Go away."

He opened the door and came in. He was dressed in gray trousers and a white shirt. Evidently he'd used one of the other bathrooms on that floor to bathe and dress for dinner.

He stood beside the bed, his hands in his trouser pockets. "Mala says you're not feeling well."

"Surprise!" said Susan scornfully.

His lips thinned. "Do you feel like talking?"

"No." She hesitated, then said, "On second thought, yes. One of us is going to move out of this bedroom. Who?"

His breath escaped from his mouth in a small explosion. "We aren't going to settle anything that way."

"Everything is already settled, except for deciding who will use this room. If you don't want to move to the other end of the hall, I will. It makes not a bit of difference to me."

He uttered a curse. "Since you're already situated here, I'll sleep elsewhere—for the time being."

"And bathe and dress and whatever else you do. As long as I am in this house this is my room and I don't want anyone coming in here without my permission."

"You're behaving like a child!"

She pulled the sheet over her and turned away from him. "That's all I have to say to you, Travis. Whenever you decide a divorce is the only sensible alternative for us, let me know. Good night."

Although he said nothing, she felt him standing there for several long moments, looking at her and breathing hard. Finally, he walked out, slamming the door behind him. Susan turned on her back again and took a weak, shuddering breath. She was trembling. She got up and looked around the room, finally carrying a chair over to the door and wedging its back under the doorknob.

Standing back, she looked at what she had done, and a sudden hysterical laugh threatened to push its way from her throat. She *was* being a bit melodramatic. But she left the chair where it was.

She didn't sleep, except for brief, fitful dozes, until dawn.

A week later, she went downstairs for dinner. In the past seven days, she had only been out of her room during the daylight hours when she knew Travis was gone. Mala had been bringing her her dinner on a tray and looking more perplexed and worried as the days passed, for after the first forty-eight hours Susan's cold symptoms had disappeared.

She had been bolstering her resolve and gathering her courage, and tonight she had decided she wasn't going to be a prisoner in the house any longer. She was going to go on with her life as if nothing had happened, except with Travis. Him, she would continue to ignore as much as possible. She was determined to wait him out; she could live in an armed camp as long as he could, she told herself.

She arrived in the dining room just as Mala was placing Travis's salad in front of him. "Oh, Miz Susan!" Mala seemed glad to see her. It was impossible to tell what Travis felt, not that she cared. She took a chair at the opposite end of the table from her husband and Mala brought in her salad.

"This must mean you're feeling more yourself," Travis observed.

Susan glanced at him, but did not answer. She added dressing to her salad and began to eat.

"You may remember that we discussed sending out marriage announcements," he went on in a dogged voice. "I had them engraved and mailed them yesterday."

Susan looked up. "That ought to be good for a few laughs among your friends."

"Don't be ridiculous," he retorted, losing patience. "No one knows the provisions of my grandfather's will."

"Except for Curt and Violet and your dear friend, Kay."

"I've made sure that Curt and Violet won't spread it around. As for Kay, I've already spoken to her."

Susan uttered a short, humorless laugh. "Naturally. Did she commiserate with you over this dreadful farce you're forced to endure in the hope of keeping the old family plantation?"

"We didn't discuss my marriage. Kay thinks you've known about the will all along. I merely asked her not to say anything about it to anyone else. If I hadn't run into her within an hour after I'd learned about it myself, I'd never have confided in her. I was stunned and not in control of my judgment."

"Harris Sennett must have been a sly old codger to have pulled the wool over your eyes so completely. It's a characteristic that seems to run in the family."

For a moment she saw something like grief in

his eyes, and then it was gone. "I'm sorry, Susan. There's no excuse for my not telling you about the will before we married."

"Of course there is. If you *had*, there never would have *been* a marriage."

"Can't we try to put that behind us now and—"

"I don't believe this, Travis!" she exploded. "What do you take me for? I may have been deluded for a while, but I'm not stupid. If you really want to keep your inheritance, you'd better agree to a quick divorce and find another patsy before it's too late."

He half rose from his chair as Amii came into the room with the main course. He sat down abruptly and the maid eyed him curiously. When Amii was gone, he said, "There will be no divorce."

"Fine," said Susan sharply. "Nor will there be an heir. I happen to have control over that."

He stared at her, his eyes swimming with anger. "There's always adoption."

She gasped. "No reputable agency would give you a child without my consent. What kind of environment would this be? And if you think I won't make my opposition known, you're dead wrong."

"There are ways," he stated grimly.

She gave him a contemptuous look and turned her attention to her meal. After some moments, he said, "We're invited to a dinner party tomorrow evening. Jonathan Wicksham, a man I've known for a number of years, is giving it."

"You can make my apologies."

"You're going with me. The party is in our honor." His mouth twisted wryly. "A little celebration for the happy newlyweds."

"I'm not the hypocrite you are," she told him. "I don't think I can play the adoring wife."

"You will," Travis said. "If you're not ready to go by eight o'clock tomorrow night, I'll dress you myself and carry you to the car. We're going to start appearing in public together, and we will present a united front. Don't oppose me in this, Susan."

"Or what?" she inquired, trembling. "You'll beat me into submission?"

He merely stared at her with disdain and began to talk about the cane harvest. Susan remained stonily silent for the remainder of the meal, and when Amii came in with dessert, she shook her head and left the table.

After Travis's warning, she gave very little thought to staying away from Jonathan Wicksham's party. She had heard the stubborness in Travis's tone and believed he would force her to go if she balked. She might kick and scream, but she shrank from playing out a scene like that with him. She preferred being ready at eight the next evening in an appropriate dress of pale blue summer crepe, her hair freshly shampooed and brushed back into a chic coil secured with pearl-studded combs, so that she could face Travis and his friends with dignity.

On the drive into Bridgetown, Travis told her that Jonathan Wicksham was a wealthy widower with financial interests on the island. She was prepared to dislike the man, along with all of Travis's other friends, but when he turned out to be a charming, white-haired gentleman in his late fifties who gave her an effusive, and clearly sincere, welcome, she found herself warming to him.

Jonathan's home was a stately old mansion enclosed by a high stone wall and furnished with lovely French and Italian antiques. The other guests had already arrived, and Susan and Travis were immediately surrounded. Travis seemed perfectly at ease as he introduced her, his arm around her waist possessively. She thought, What a consummate actor he is!

As cocktails were being served in the huge, chandeliered living room, Kay Harte sat down beside Susan. "Travis tells me you've been under the weather. Nothing serious, I hope."

Susan searched her face for signs of smugness or gloating, but Kay's brown eyes looked directly into hers with an openness that she did not think could be feigned. "Only a cold."

"It's probably because your system hasn't adjusted to our climate yet. The humidity is oppressive at times—especially to newcomers. You'll get used to it."

Not if I have my way, Susan thought. She still hoped that Travis would agree to a divorce before very long. She saw him watching her uneasily from across the room, probably wondering what she was saying to Kay, and realized that she could make him more uncomfortable in public than in private. His insistence that they be seen together was bound to put him under a strain.

She smiled brightly at Kay, feeling Travis's eyes still on her. "I'm sure you're right. Tell me, do you have any new merchandise since my visit to the boutique?"

"I received a shipment of evening dresses yesterday. You must come in soon before they're all picked over."

Susan chatted with Kay until it was time to go in for dinner, pretending to be engrossed in their talk about the latest styles from Paris. When Jonathan Wicksham appeared to ask for the honor of escorting her to table, Susan accepted. Seated on Jonathan's right, with Travis between Kay and another woman at the other end of the large table, Susan smiled and flirted openly with her host throughout the long meal.

By the time they left the table, Travis's face was tight and his glance, whenever she met it, was fuming.

Susan returned to the living room on Jonathan's arm and sat down with him in a private corner. Other conversational groups formed about them and spilled over into adjoining rooms. As the evening progressed, Susan was never unaware of the close watch Travis was keeping on her, and she laughed and flirted even more. Eventually, she became aware that some of the other guests were also watching her and Jonathan with raised eyebrows.

"You have a lovely home," Susan said, looking into her host's light gray eyes.

"Yes, isn't it? It's very old and had been allowed to deteriorate lamentably before I purchased it five years ago. I've tried to restore it to its former beauty—with a few modern additions, of course."

Susan glanced about the gracious living room.

"You've done a marvelous job. Are you in the decorating business?"

"Not as a profession. I've studied all that I could find about the architecture and decor of the finest early Barbadian homes in order to make my restoration here authentic, though." He smiled warmly at her. "I'm flattered that you approve of what I've done. Of course, Travis has another fine example of the old great houses."

"Yes," Susan murmured, "it's a beautiful place."

"Will you be doing any redecorating?"

"I don't think so."

"Well, if you decide to and I can be of any help to you, don't hesitate to ask."

"Thank you, Jonathan. I'll remember that." She accepted a glass of champagne from a tray offered by a uniformed maid. "So, you're not in the decorating business. What *do* you do?"

"I'm semiretired now. I have investments in various enterprises here and in other places in the Caribbean. Overseeing them doesn't take up a great deal of my time, however. How are you occupying yourself since coming to Barbados?"

"I'm reading about the history of your island. Next I intend to explore the places I've read about."

"Perhaps you will allow me to accompany you on some of your jaunts?"

Susan sipped the excellent champagne and smiled at him. "I'd be delighted for your company. Give me a ring when you have a free day." She glanced aside to see Travis bearing down on them.

"Jonathan, thank you for your hospitality."

Travis extended his hand to the other man, who was getting to his feet. "I'm afraid we have to be leaving now. Susan has been a little unwell the past few days, and I don't want her to become overtired."

Susan set her glass aside and got to her feet to clasp their host's hand. "Thank you, Jonathan. I can't think when I've enjoyed myself more than I have tonight." She looked directly at Travis as she said this.

Then he was gripping her arm and they were crossing the room, to be stopped several times by other guests who said they were pleased to have met Susan and promised that the Sennetts would be receiving more invitations soon.

Susan managed to reply to one and all graciously but, by the time she and Travis were in the car, her face felt stiff from so many false smiles.

Instead of starting the motor immediately, Travis gripped the steering wheel and said through clenched teeth, "I could kill you."

"Spoken like a devoted husband," Susan said, her tone as grim as his own.

"I never saw such a sickening display in my life!"

Susan glanced coldly at his rigid profile. "Whatever are you talking about?"

He seemed to be trying to break the steering wheel in two. "Is that your idea of revenge, flirting with Jonathan Wicksham all evening under my nose? You acted like a—cheap floozy."

"But, Travis," she said with acid sweetness, "I was merely being nice to one of your friends. Isn't that what you wanted me to do?"

"Jonathan Wicksham is no friend of mine—not after tonight, at any rate." He let go of the wheel and turned toward her. His eyes glowed with a dangerous fire in the shadowed planes of his face.

"That's between you and Jonathan, but I'll choose my own friends."

Roughly, he reached out and grabbed her arms. "You little—" His face was cold above hers, his eyes hard. She stared at him and began to struggle. His head came down, and his mouth took hers in a cruel, possessive kiss, grinding the tender skin inside her mouth against her teeth.

She jerked her head back and a dull pain shot through her neck. She choked with impotent fury. The sound of their heavy breathing was loud in the car. "Let me go, Travis," she said in a low, breathless voice, "or I'll start screaming. Some of your friends are coming out of the house now. Do you want them to see the newlyweds brawling?"

A muscle alongside his mouth jerked, betraying his banked rage. He let her go, started the engine and slammed the car into gear. Neither of them spoke during the drive and, as soon as the car had stopped at the house, Susan shoved her door open, stepped out and ran up the front steps.

In her room, the chair once again wedged beneath the knob, she sat down on the bed and tried to stop the trembling of her limbs. She despised Travis, longed to hit him, hurt him, until her fury had been released. Yet part of her seething anger was directed inward, at herself, because for a brief moment when he was kissing her she had felt that familiar, awful weakness. She sensed that if his friends had not come outside, if he had not stopped that brutally passionate kiss, something in her would have been ignited and he would have proved his mastery over her once more. Above all else, that must not happen now, or she would lose whatever bargaining power she had with him.

Her breathing steadier, she undressed and got into bed. So he thought he could overcome her resistance, did he? He thought he could shame her, destroy her pride, force her to bear his child and go on with a life together just as he had planned. Susan tossed restlessly on her bed. Because of the ease with which he had convinced her to marry him, he no doubt thought her a delicate, spineless female who could not stand up under the force of his will. He'd find out otherwise. Oh, yes, he surely would find out!

She had not even *begun* to make his life unbearable. But tonight she had seen the path she must take to bring him to his knees, begging for a divorce.

Two days later, when Jonathan Wicksham telephoned to ask her to go for a drive about the island, she agreed with alacrity, then spent an hour making herself as attractive as possible. She wore a white batiste sundress with wide lace inserts banding the full skirt, white high-heeled spaghetti-strap sandals and dangling white hoop earrings that were exposed provocatively whenever she tossed back her long, silver-blond hair.

At three, as she left the house, she called to Mala not to wait dinner on her, since she had no idea when she would be home. Jonathan handed her into the back seat of a black Rolls Royce and got in beside her. He gave directions to his driver, then settled against the plush upholstery to run his eyes over her.

"You look incredibly beautiful—like a carefree young nymph."

She tucked her hand through the bend of his elbow. "Thank you, Jonathan. Where are you taking me?"

"I thought we'd start with Sam Lord's Castle. You look as if you belong in a castle."

She smiled and relaxed in the comfortable seat. "I haven't run across it in my reading. Tell me about it."

"Alas, it's become a resort hotel in recent years—but very posh, one of the nicest and most expensive on the island. Of course, it was never a real castle. Actually, it's a Georgian mansion built by the notorious buccaneer Samuel Lord who, legend has it, used to hang lanterns in the coconut trees along a rocky stretch of shoreline. Ship captains mistook them for the lights of Bridgetown and crashed on the reef. Then Sam helped himself to their cargo. He became a very wealthy man."

"You almost sound as if you admire him," said Susan with a chuckle.

"I admire enterprise in anyone, not that I approve of Sam's method of making his way in the world. I do approve of his taste for the finer things in life, however. I studied his mansion and the furnishings closely when I was restoring my own house. The Castle possesses many priceless antiques—furniture, paintings, silver, china. And wait until you see the ornate stucco work on the ceilings. One of them is a copy of a ceiling in Windsor Castle."

During the drive, he pointed out a few other old mansions that had once been plantation great houses, like the one on the Sennett Plantation. It was evident that he knew a great deal about Barbados and its early settlers.

"You should write a history of the island," Susan told him. "I'm learning more from you than I am from the books I bought in Bridgetown. You make it seem more real somehow."

"The difference is probably that I truly love Barbados and grieve for the way it has been plundered by some of those who've lived here."

"You mean the slaveholders?"

"Yes, and I'm afraid the same sort of people are still with us today. They're descendants of the old families who nearly ruined the island's economy by amassing vast quantities of land for their own selfish purposes."

"Like the Sennetts," Susan murmured.

He darted an apologetic look at her. "Forgive me, Susan. What abominable manners I have! Here I sit, criticizing your husband's family after you so graciously consented to share your afternoon with me."

"No, don't apologize. I really do want to learn what I can about Barbados—the bad as well as the good. I know that Travis owns a great deal of land, but why do you disapprove?"

"The problem is, my dear, that Barbados is so small—little more than a hundred fifty square miles, and not all of that, even apart from the space the towns occupy, is tillable." He seemed to speak guardedly, as if he were afraid of offending her. "Do you understand what I'm saying? In your vast country, thousands of acres can be appropriated by one person without harm to others. Here, though, the effect of having large tracts held by a few families is that the poor are denied land ownership and the pride that comes with self-sufficiency." He gave her hand a quick squeeze. "Now, that's enough of dreary polemic for one day. Sam Lord's Castle is just around the next bend."

The Castle, situated on the southeast coast of the island facing the Atlantic, lived up to Jonathan's description of it. It was built of stone with massive walls and crenellated battlements, painted entirely white, with open verandas all around the building. The lawns and gardens, with fountains and great beds of bright oleanders, hibiscus, ginger lilies and other native flowers, created a beautiful park. The second floor contained guest rooms, but the ground floor had been kept open for visitors, dozens of whom were touring it at the same time that Jonathan showed Susan around.

They left an hour later and made several other stops before dark when Jonathan asked, "Do I dare hope you will have dinner with me in Bridgetown before I take you home?"

"I'd like that very much," Susan said, imagining Travis, who should be having his own dinner about now, listening for the sound of a car and watching the door for her return.

Jonathan took her to a small, intimate restaurant on a Bridgetown side street where the chef specialized in French cuisine. It was after ten when they returned to the plantation and Susan said, "You needn't come in with me. Thank you, Jonathan dear, for a wonderful day."

"I should thank you," he assured her. "I hope we'll be able to do it again soon."

"So do I." She got out of the car and stood for a minute, watching the Rolls pull smoothly away from the house.

Travis met her at the foot of the stairs. "Where the hell have you been?"

"With Jonathan Wicksham. Didn't Mala tell you?"

He snorted with disgust. "She said you left with him at three this afternoon. What were you doing all this time?"

She shrugged carelessly. "Sightseeing, having dinner. I really can't give you a minute-by-minute account, Travis. I'm tired and want to go to bed."

She started up the stairs, but he caught her arm, whirling her about to face him. "Listen to me! I don't trust Wicksham, and neither should you."

Her tone was icy. "You'll forgive me if I can't put much stock in that opinion, considering the source."

His fingers pressed into the skin of her upper arm painfully. "You can't fool me," he rasped. "I know what you're up to with Wicksham, but don't waste your time."

It was only with the utmost effort that she held her ground, glaring at him. She felt taut as a wire and she saw that he stood in much the same way as she—tight, barely controlled, an invisible but palpable charge sparking between them. She sensed that he would like nothing better than for her to struggle to be free of his grip. That would give him an excuse to demonstrate his superior strength. The thought helped cool her seething emotions.

She smiled stiffly. "I don't know what you're talking about."

"Yes, you do," he snapped. "You think that if you traipse all over Barbados, making a fool of yourself with another man, I'll give in to your demands. But I won't. *There will be no divorce!* Is that understood?"

"Perfectly," she retorted sarcastically.

"Fine." He let her go so abruptly that she almost lost her footing. "Good night."

Susan ran up the stairs and barricaded herself in her bedroom. She began to undress, flinging her clothes stormily across the bed.

What a hateful man he was! How could she have been so blind to his true character in the beginning? Well, whatever had overcome her intelligence and good judgment, she was seeing things clearly now. The thought of his repeated refusals to give her a divorce and allow her to leave Barbados made her burn all over. But she knew that she *had* bothered him by going out with Jonathan, no matter what he said. So she would continue her campaign with renewed determination.

Chapter Eight

During the next few weeks, Susan went out with Jonathan at least twice a week. He was a very comfortable companion, and the times she spent with him became the only bright spots in her life, the only thing she looked forward to with any eagerness. She had come to think of Jonathan as a dear friend. At first, Travis met her when Jonathan returned her to the house, resentful, demanding an explanation as to where she'd been. Susan always treated his questions with cool disdain, as if she were dealing with a particularly offensive casual acquaintance. The rest of the time when she was with Travis, he remained surly and uncommunicative.

One night, after Susan had gone to Jonathan's house for a quiet dinner for two and returned even later than usual, Travis stormed into her bedroom. Since he hadn't met her at the door, she had decided he'd given up interrogating her about what she did when she left the house. She should have known he wouldn't give up so easily.

She had already gotten into her gown and was

in bed, glancing through a guidebook Jonathan had loaned her. She hadn't barricaded her door for more than two weeks, having become convinced that Travis wasn't going to seek entrance, as she had feared at first.

He began to pace back and forth beside her bed like a caged animal. She lowered her book and lifted her chin.

"We're going to talk, Susan," he said shortly.

"Oh?" Her tone was disinterested, cool.

"Where did you go with Wicksham tonight?"

"To dinner."

His gold-flecked eyes flashed. *"Where?"*

"Jonathan's house," she snapped. "Does it really make any difference where we ate?"

"Yes, it does!" he thundered. "Don't you care how this looks to others—being alone with him at his house? There's only one conclusion people can draw."

"Frankly, I don't care what people think."

He flushed under his tan. "Are you going to go on punishing me for the rest of our lives? Do you enjoy watching me suffer? Or is it just that you've found a bigger goldmine, someone who's free to dance attendance on you whenever you crook a finger, someone who has more money than your husband? Are you trying to line up a husband number two, Susan?"

"You're disgusting!" Susan cried hotly. "You're hateful and vile to say a thing like that to me! Only *you* would see something self-serving in a simple friendship!"

"Don't make me laugh," he growled. *"Friendship!* Wicksham doesn't know the meaning of the word."

Seething with indignation, Susan retorted, "How would you know? The only way you know how to treat people is to use them! You're the biggest hypocrite on God's green earth! You told me you wanted me to have friends, you introduced me to Jonathan, and now you're determined to destroy the only friendship I have here."

"You could have other friends, but you won't give anyone else a chance. Kay's told me she's called to ask you to lunch twice, and both times you made up some excuse."

"Did it ever occur to you," Susan cried, "that I don't want to be friends with your lovers? Your precious, smug Kay makes me sick! Jonathan is a gentle, considerate man and he understands me, which is more than I can say for you."

Travis strode toward her, anger tightening the muscles of his bronzed face. "Gentle! Considerate! You're even more foolish than I thought. Don't you know that Wicksham is using you to get at me?" He was leaning over her now, his eyes burning like gold-flecked coals.

Tears sprang into Susan's eyes. "Naturally. Everything revolves around you, doesn't it, Travis? You never loved me! You don't even love poor Kay, even though it's obvious she's been eating her heart out for you for years! You despise any man who befriends me. The only thing you ever think about is *you*—and what you want. And you don't care how many people you have to hurt to get it." Her hand lashed out. She wanted to batter him, to claw at his face, to hurt him as he had hurt her.

Travis caught her wrist in an iron grip before

her hand made contact with his flesh. He loomed over her, his expression grim with fury. "Woman, you don't know the first thing about what I think or want, and you know even less about a man like Wicksham."

"I know that he's my friend," she shot back. "I don't care what you think he is. Nothing he's ever done could be as bad as what you've done to me. You've ruined my life!"

He laughed harshly, coming down against her. "I made you my wife, took you away from a life that you'd become disillusioned with, gave you my home. Is that how I ruined your life?" She could feel his muscles through the sheet and their clothing. A betraying tremor shook her body.

Refusing to acknowledge what she felt, Susan whispered hoarsely, "I despise you!" She tried to twist away from him, but his arms came around her, clamping her against him. She pushed at the bulk of his chest, frantic to free herself.

Heat flamed in his eyes, and for a moment Susan was still, caught by the fire of his gaze. Slowly, deliberately, his head came down. His lips brushed hers, at first softly, then with increasing pressure, until his mouth was devouring hers.

She felt herself drowning, her will dissolving away. He had not touched her in such a long time, a lifetime it seemed. He had never said that he loved her, although at first she had accepted tender words spoken in the heat of passion as expressions of love. He certainly did not even say that he loved her now, and yet she trembled in his arms, melted at his touch.

His arms loosened their grip, and one hand slid down to stroke her neck and roam over her breasts. In a last desperate attempt to assert her will, she tore her mouth from his and turned her head away. With a sob, she choked out, "I won't let you do this to me! Get out! Leave me alone!"

"You want me as much as I want you," he said, his voice low and throbbing.

"No! I don't want you!"

"Ah, I see." His voice held soft menace. "Are you sleeping with Wicksham now? Is that why you have no need for your husband?"

She kept her head turned away from him and swallowed hard. She forced her voice to be steady. If she gave in to him now, she would never be free of the hold he had on her emotions. "What Jonathan and I do is none of your business. You wouldn't understand, anyway, so I won't even try to tell you. But no matter what you think, I don't want you. I never will again." She turned her head and looked into his eyes. "You can rape me, but you can't make me respond to you."

He stiffened at her words and his face contorted. Abruptly, he moved off her, getting to his feet. Then, with a muttered curse, he turned and left the room. After he was gone, she stared at the closed door and, inside, she seethed and hurt, feeling empty and unfulfilled.

After several moments, she picked up the discarded guidebook and tried to read. But it was no use. She couldn't concentrate on the words, couldn't think of anything but Travis, the terrible things he had said to her, and the way he could make her want him in spite of all that had happened between them. It was much later when she finally slept.

She awoke the next morning with a slight queasy sensation. Sure that the feeling was the result of the heated exchange she and Travis had had the night before and her subsequent inability to sleep well, she got up, confident that the queasiness would leave when she started to move about. But the sudden movement made her stomach feel as if it were turning wrong side out and climbing into her throat, and she ran to the bathroom where she lost what little remained in her stomach. Then she was wracked by dry heaves that left her shaking and exhausted. When her stomach quieted, she crept back to bed and sank down between the sheets, feeling as if she weighed a ton.

Although her body was incapable, for the moment, of anything but weak, settling movements, her mind was working frantically. She had been married for six weeks and, although she tried desperately to convince herself otherwise, she finally admitted that her monthly cycle had not come around since her wedding day.

She knew that worry and strain and other emotional upheavals could throw a woman's system off temporarily. She had even heard of women who experienced a full nine months of false pregnancy because they wanted a child so badly. But she did not want a child—quite the opposite. She might have been able to convince herself that tension had caused some sort of hormonal imbalance if it weren't for the nausea. That, added to the fact that she had taken no precautions against pregnancy, left only one conclusion, and she unwillingly admitted it into her consciousness, hearing the words in her mind: *I'm carrying Travis's child.*

Even then she immediately pushed the thought away, refusing to deal with it—yet hardly able to think of anything else. Other things could cause nausea, she told herself. Perhaps something she had eaten at Jonathan's the night before had disagreed with her. Perhaps she was coming down with a virus.

But when she suffered from morning queasiness for the next three days in a row, she could no longer hang on to even a remote doubt that she was pregnant.

Again, she stopped having dinner with Travis, telling Mala that she preferred eating earlier, that she became too hungry if she waited until eight. In fact, she was avoiding being in the same room with her husband even more assiduously than before. She had a desperate fear that Travis would see a change in her and guess the cause. If that happened, she would be lost. He would never allow her to leave him while she was carrying his child.

After several days of this, her nerves were in shreds. When Jonathan came to take her out for an early dinner one evening, she practically ran out of the house, so eager was she to be free of its heavy oppression.

When they were seated in the little Bridgetown restaurant where they had dined several times before, Jonathan's concerned gaze moved slowly over her.

"Well, I'm going to say it, and you can tell me

to mind my own business if you wish. You look wretched, my dear. You're as beautiful as ever, but those dark circles under your eyes weren't there the last time I saw you. And your face has a drawn look. I hope you aren't on one of those silly crash diets that women always seem to punish themselves with. You don't have an extra ounce of weight on you that I can see."

Susan reached for her water glass and lifted it to her mouth. Her hand trembled. She set the glass down and shook her head. "I'm not dieting. I haven't been feeling well."

He reached across the table and took her cold fingers in his. "I haven't wanted to say anything, Susan, but it's been evident for some time that you're unhappy. Is there anything I can do to help?"

The sweet kindness in his silver-gray eyes undid her. Tears sprang into her eyes and she had to blink repeatedly to keep them from spilling down her face. She pulled her hand away and dabbed at her eyes with her napkin. "You— you're the only friend I have, Jonathan. I—I don't know what I'd do without you."

He waited, his compassionate gaze urging her to confide in him. She drew an uneven breath. "My marriage is a mess," she finally said, the words tumbling past the knot of tears in her throat. "Travis only married me because of his grandfather's will."

"I don't know what you're talking about, but I'm sure you must have misjudged Travis. He and I don't always see eye to eye, but he'd have to be a fool not to love you."

Susan saw the irony in Jonathan's defending

Travis, when Travis had nothing but cutting sarcasm for Jonathan. She smiled shakily. "No, you're wrong. Harris Sennett attached a condition to Travis's continued ownership of the plantation and the bank. He must have a legitimate heir by the time he's thirty-five or lose everything."

For once, she thought she had truly shocked the sophisticated Jonathan. "But—that's preposterous." He was shaking his head. "Harris wouldn't do a thing like that. He had that air of superiority that always seems to mark members of the old families. He would have wanted his holdings to remain in Sennett hands, Travis's hands. The thought of anyone else acquiring anything that had been in the family so long would have been totally unacceptable to him."

Susan shrugged helplessly. "I don't know the details, but evidently, if there is no heir, Travis's cousins will come into part—or all—of the Barbados holdings."

He was frowning. "Forgive me, Susan, but why did you marry him, knowing this?"

She swallowed convulsively. "I didn't know it—until afterward. I'm sure Travis would have kept me in ignorance from now on but . . . other people let things slip."

He sighed. "Ah, the cousins. I haven't met them, but I've heard they're staying in town."

"Travis threw them out of the house."

His laugh was humorless. "No doubt he feared just what happened—that they would give him away." He held her gaze for a long moment. "My dear Susan, why don't you leave him?"

She shook her head, unable to speak for a

moment, not willing to reveal, even to Jonathan, what Travis had threatened to do should she try to leave. Finally, she said, "I . . . I can't leave—yet. At first, I held onto the belief that I would get away from him and find a job. But now, everything has changed." Fresh tears blurred her vision. "Oh, Jonathan, I'm pregnant and I—I don't know what I'm going to do."

He took both her hands in an effort to comfort her. "You poor child. Does Travis know?"

"No! And he mustn't, at least, not until I decide what I am to do."

"Abortion?" The word was low.

She stared at him. "I've thought of it. But what doctor here would do it without notifying Travis first? He's too influential for any of them to consider performing an abortion without his knowledge. Besides, no matter how much I despise Travis, I don't think I could do that to his child—my child, too."

"I suspect," he said sadly, "that you're still in love with him."

"No," she said emphatically. "I'm not—I won't be. All I need is time to recover from him. Please, promise me that you'll tell no one about my pregnancy."

He smiled. "I swear it. And—" he made a small dismissive gesture with one hand—"if you change your mind about an abortion, there are ways to accomplish it in secrecy. I have contacts of my own here. One can always find a doctor who has something to hide—or who needs money very badly. Provided you don't wait too long."

She shivered, thinking of dark and dirty back

rooms. "Thank you, but I won't change my mind. I'll have to find another way out of the mess I've made of my life."

"You're a brave woman," he said earnestly. The waiter came then and took their order, and Jonathan, with a sensitivity to her feelings, turned the conversation deftly to other things.

Later, when they left the restaurant, they walked along the narrow side street to where Jonathan's car and driver waited. Even with Jonathan beside her, Susan couldn't help feeling a little uneasy about their surroundings. Once one left the main thoroughfares of Bridgetown, the streets and alleyways quickly deteriorated into slums where rickety shacks crowded against the street and each other, their inhabitants spilling out of them to sit or lie in front or mill aimlessly about the street.

"These people," she remarked in a low tone, "seem so restless and unhappy."

"What you see is desperation," he told her. "Most of them have no jobs and little hope of finding one. There isn't even room for a vegetable garden here, which would help put food on the table. These are the people who suffer from the unequal division of our precious land."

Susan remained quiet during the drive home, brooding over the poor people she had seen, wondering how they could continue to live without hope or purpose.

She was in a depressed mood when she entered the house, wanting only to crawl into bed and drown the memory of the slum in sleep. But Travis was waiting for her and, over her feeble protests, steered her into the living room, where he poured a glass of wine and handed it to her.

"Drink this. You look pale," he said tersely. "I suppose dear friend Jonathan is beginning to grate on your nerves. How you've managed to endure him this long, I can't think."

She didn't deny it, preferring that he blame Jonathan for her paleness rather than guess the true reason. She sank into a chair and sipped the wine, feeling its slow warmth creeping along her veins.

He stood over her, looking stern and uncompromising. "Have you been to Wicksham's house again?"

She wasn't up to playing devious games. "No, we went to a restaurant."

"It's obvious you're in poor spirits. What happened? If he hurt you—"

She cut in scathingly. "Stop playing the outraged husband, Travis. Jonathan was the soul of consideration, as usual. If my spirits seem low, perhaps it's because I got a good look at the people who live in one of your Bridgetown slums." She shuddered and took a swallow of wine. "There must be thousands of people like that, rotting on Barbados, without jobs, stripped of whatever dignity they may once have had. Jonathan says there's no hope for them as long as people like you hoard all the wealth."

He threw back his head and laughed. "Oh, Lord, that's rich! But I can't believe you're naive enough to fall for that old line. You've seen Wicksham's house. Have you any idea how much wealth it took to restore it and furnish it?

He has other houses, too, on other islands. He's one of the richest men in the West Indies. What is *he* doing to help the poor?"

"I don't know," she retorted, suddenly too tired to pursue an argument with him. "More than you, I'm sure. At least, he doesn't own acres and acres of land."

"You couldn't be more wrong," he grated.

She finished her wine and got to her feet with a great effort of will; all she wanted to do was to put her head back and go to sleep on the spot. Did pregnancy sap the energy from all women, or only those who were caught in unhappy marriages? "I don't think so, Travis, but we aren't going to solve this particular disagreement tonight. I'm going to bed."

He stood in front of her, blocking her way. "Not just yet. I have something to tell you first."

She was immediately on the alert, tensely anticipating a sudden movement from him. If he touched her now, enfolded her in the strength and warmth of his arms, she wasn't sure she could fight him. She felt too helpless and vulnerable.

"What is it?"

"The work here is caught up temporarily. We're going to have a few slow days before anymore of the cane will be ready for harvest. I want us to go away together for a week." He was watching her intently. "Call it the honeymoon we never had."

It was too much, on top of everything else, for him to stand there with that implacable stubbornness stiffening every muscle in his body and talk to her about a honeymoon—as if they

had a real marriage, as if he were the least bit
concerned about her and her happiness. She
almost choked on her resentment. "Is this your
idea of a joke? Do you think I could stand being
alone with you for a full week? Dear heaven,
Travis! Must you make my life more miserable
at every turn?"

"That wasn't my intention," he stated curtly.
"You're looking too tense lately. It will do us
both good to get away from the plantation."

"The only way I want to leave the plantation is
alone and bound for the States."

"I have the use of a beach cottage on the other
side of the island," he went on, as if she hadn't
spoken. "We'll leave in the morning."

What little blood was left in her face drained
out of it and she staggered slightly. He caught
her arm, frowning. "Are you all right?"

She gritted her teeth and drew in several
gulps of air to clear her swimming head. "No, I
am not all right. And I will not be all right until
I'm free of you. If you imagine for one minute
that we can have a honeymoon—in the true
sense of that word—you're insane. You can keep
me imprisoned in a beach cottage for the rest of
our natural lives, and I'll still feel nothing but
disgust when you touch me." She twisted away
from him and walked out of the room on unsteady legs. He did not try to stop her.

But he didn't change his mind about going
away, either. When she came downstairs for
breakfast the next morning, he was idling at the
table over a cup of coffee, the remains of scrambled eggs on his plate.

"Good morning, Susan. I trust you rested well.

You're looking better than you did last night, at any rate."

She helped herself to eggs and a biscuit from a warming tray, and he finished his coffee before he said, "Can you be ready to leave in an hour?"

She looked into his dark eyes and knew that he had made up his mind to take her to that detestable beach cottage no matter what she said. She sighed, thinking that she would take an armload of books so that she could spend the days reading. Let him swim and walk along the beach to his heart's content, as long as he left her alone. "Yes," she said shortly.

There was a noticeable relaxing of the muscles in his face. "Good. You won't need anything but swimwear and shorts. We won't be going out or seeing anybody."

She merely nodded and began to eat her breakfast. For the past few mornings, the sickness had not been so bad, and as she thought of this, she told herself glumly: *Be grateful for small favors since you're not likely to receive any large ones.*

After breakfast, she threw a few things into a small suitcase and followed Travis to the car. His face was set, as if her clear lack of enthusiasm was beginning to strain his patience. She hoped so. Maybe he would be bored enough to come back home before the week was over.

They drove south, the opposite direction from Bridgetown. Travis turned on the car radio, picking up the island's only station, and plaintive Polynesian music thrummed about them. He spoke only occasionally, to point out something of interest, but did not seem to expect any answers from her. Soon, in spite of her resistance to the trip, Susan began to feel less resentful, more relaxed. It *was* good to get away from the house for a few days, even in the company of Travis.

"This is Ragged Point," Travis said as they came around a sharp curve, the road overlooking a sheer cliff and turbulent waters below. A lighthouse perched on a jutting prominence. "There's a very dangerous reef here known as The Cobblers," Travis went on. "Supposedly, this is the spot where a notorious pirate named Sam Lord lured sailors onto the rocks with lanterns."

"Oh, are we near Sam Lord's Castle?"

He glanced at her. "Yes. You've heard of it?"

"Jonathan took me to see it."

She saw his lips clamp together, as if he were keeping in angry words, and she wished that she hadn't mentioned Jonathan. She couldn't bear this trip if they were to be at sword's points all the time. She made an attempt to divert his attention. "This is a beautiful view from up here."

He remained silent for a moment, then said, "We're in St. John's Parish now. The church is one of the nicest on the island. Would you like to see it?"

She found herself agreeing, thinking that the longer they delayed reaching their destination, the longer it would be before she would be sharing the intimacy of a beach cottage with Travis.

The church sat on the edge of the cliff overlooking the east coast; a sign informed passersby that they were 825 feet above sea level. The building was of the same gray-colored stones as the church she had visited in Bridgetown, but here no town buildings or traffic detracted from its lovely isolation. The grounds were large and well kept. They got out of the car and strolled toward the church.

"An older church was destroyed by a hurricane in 1831," Travis said. "This one was completed a few years later. A descendant of Constantine the Great, of Turkey, is buried in this churchyard. He came here after his family was driven from Constantinople. Want to have a look at his gravestone?"

Susan agreed and they walked among the old graves, along with a few other visitors, until they found the moss-encrusted marker where the name "Ferdinando Paleologus" was almost obscured. Inside, the church was cool and modestly furnished. A woman was kneeling at the altar. Unwilling to intrude, they stood at the back and looked around without talking, and Susan felt an almost palpable atmosphere of peace, so much so that she was reluctant to leave when Travis touched her arm and gestured toward the door.

When they were in the car again, she asked suddenly, "Was your family Anglican?" She had never wondered before.

"Yes. My grandmother was quite devout, I've been told, although she died when I was too young to remember her. There are churches closer to the plantation than St. John's, but I've always thought I'd like to have my own children baptized here."

Susan looked at him quickly, but the remark was evidently a casual one with no hidden meanings. Yet she would not have guessed that Travis had any religious feelings whatever. "How far are we from the cottage?"

"Only a few miles now."

All too soon, Travis turned the car down a narrow, descending road and stopped beside a small, isolated, wind-whitened dwelling. He took a key from his pocket and opened the door, and Susan followed him inside.

In contrast to the outside, which the elements had weathered severely, the interior was attractive and colorful, the walls painted pale yellow, flowered curtains at the windows. The wood floors shone with the deep patina of many waxings, and there were bright-colored rag rugs scattered about. There was a central room with rattan couches and chairs, padded with cotton cushions in blue and green, at one end and a small kitchen at the other. A round maple table and chairs separated the two areas. Susan breathed easier when she saw that there were two bedrooms opening off the main room. A third door led into a bath.

Travis set their suitcases down beside a couch. "Do you like it?"

"It's very cheery," she admitted.

"It was nice of Kay to offer to loan it to us for a week."

The knowledge that it was Kay Harte's cottage did not set well with Susan, although she made no comment. She couldn't help wondering, though, if Travis and Kay had ever stayed here together. She found that she resented that thought and pushed it away. She picked up her small case.

"I'll take this bedroom," she said, "and you can have the other."

He did not respond to the obvious way she was letting him know that nothing had changed between them, even though he insisted on calling this a "honeymoon." But there was a mocking gleam in his eyes for a moment before he looked away.

"Kay said we'd find a stock of groceries in the kitchen. If we need anything else, I can drive into the nearest town." He walked over to the cabinet and was looking inside, taking inventory of the contents. Then he opened the refrigerator. "Good. Milk and eggs. Kay was here a couple of days ago. She seems to have left us well supplied." He closed the refrigerator and turned to look at her. "How about a swim before lunch?"

Susan was just beginning to realize how difficult it was going to be, staying there alone with Travis for a week, and she shook her head. "You go ahead. I think I'd rather get settled in my bedroom and read for a while."

His response was a grunt that could have meant anything, and then he lifted his suitcase and took it into one of the bedrooms. Susan entered the other and set her case on the bed. Then she sat down beside it and glanced about. The room was small, furnished with a plain pine bed and dresser, a rag rug on the floor.

She felt suddenly bereft and very much alone, as if she had come to the end of the world. Seven days of this seemed like an eternity.

Chapter Nine

*Y*ou've spent most of this holiday cooking."
Travis, from a chair at the other end of the main
room, watched her moving about the kitchen. It
was the evening of their fifth day at the cottage.

What he said was true. Desperate to fill up the
time, she had cooked two meals a day—only two
because Travis had insisted on making breakfast, saying it was the only meal simple enough
for him to handle.

She'd found a recipe book full of intriguing
sounding dishes and had driven into the nearest
town to buy ingredients that she couldn't find at
the cottage.

Although she had been doing some cooking on
the weekends lately, she had gone about it
grudgingly, resenting doing even that for Travis.
But being isolated with him in the cottage had
made her look upon the activity as a form of
salvation, and so she had lost herself for hours in
meal planning and preparation. When she
wasn't in the kitchen, she read the books she
had brought with her. After trying to coax her to
come swimming and snorkeling with him the

first two days, Travis had given in and let her be, going off for hours by himself.

"I had to have something to do," she responded as she carried an elaborate shrimp salad to the table.

Travis came to the table and eyed her creation with a pensive expression. "Looks time consuming. The making, not the eating. But this isn't exactly what I had in mind when I said you needed to get away."

Oddly, even though they had spent little time together these past few days, except for meals, Susan felt less on guard with him than at any time since she had learned about the will. She realized that this was because he had seemingly decided to keep his distance. He hadn't spoken of their relationship at all, although she had expected him to use the holiday to try to return to her bed. Now she was beginning to hope that he was considering the requested divorce.

He sampled the salad, nodding his approval. "Delicious."

"Thank you. I've never really enjoyed cooking before, but I'm discovering it can be a creative outlet."

"Must be restful, too. You're looking less tense than when we came."

"Yes . . . I think being here has helped."

"Good. I was worried about your health." He was wearing a burnt-orange ribbed-knit shirt, v'ed in front to reveal his strong, sun-bronzed neck and the beginning of dark, curling chest hair. His narrow-eyed regard made her feel too scantily clad in shorts and a strapless, elasticized knit top. She was tempted to remind him that being forced to stay married to him against her will was not exactly conducive to good health. But she didn't want to disturb the uneasy truce they seemed to have reached.

"Would you like a hot muffin?" she said to change the subject. She offered him the straw basket and he took a muffin, splitting it to add butter. They ate in silence for several moments, and Susan felt herself beginning to tighten up inside. Was it only her nerves that made the silence between them seem fraught with unspoken meanings? Why couldn't she think of something impersonal to say? The harvest! Yes, that would do. She would ask him about the cane harvest. That was a harmless enough subject.

But even as her lips parted to say the words, he broke the silence. "I'll do the dishes tonight."

"Oh, no, that isn't necessary—really."

"I insist. When you're finished eating, I want you to sit over there on the couch and watch me work for a change."

"All right." She didn't want to argue with him, certainly not over something as meaningless as who should wash the dishes. So she finished her meal and relaxed on the couch, picking up a paperback novel that lay on the floor with a page turned down to mark her place.

"I've been thinking that you might be happier if you had some work to do when we return home," Travis said as he began carrying dishes to the sink.

"What kind of work?" she asked cautiously.

"I never have enough time to keep the plantation ledgers up to date—or file anything. I bought that file cabinet in the study a year ago, intending to organize the papers that are crammed into desk drawers and bookshelves, but I still haven't found the time. It would be a big help to me if you could make some sense out of it all. You would probably do a much better job than I, since you've had some business training."

Susan put down her book. She had an impulse to retort angrily, say that she wouldn't be with him long enough to take over his office work. But, aside from the fact that he could stop her leaving without his consent, she wondered where she would go. Nobody would hire a pregnant singer, and she wouldn't be able to hide her condition after a few more weeks. The thought of going to her mother to be treated to repeated I-told-you-so lectures was almost as distasteful as staying with Travis and letting him find out about the pregnancy. But she wasn't ready to deal with those problems yet—the baby and what she would do after its birth, what Travis would allow her to do.

"Maybe I'll see what I can accomplish with your records," she ventured finally. "Once they're organized, it should be a simple matter to keep them up-to-date on a weekly basis."

He was running water in the sink and turned to look at her. Instead of meeting his look, she lifted her book again and pretended to read.

He finished the dishes and came over to the couch. "There's a cool breeze blowing in off the water. Come for a walk with me."

Realizing that he had given her no real reason to avoid him so completely since their arrival at the cottage, she felt inclined to agree. The cottage was beginning to get to her. While it was comfortable and attractive, it was also very small, and she had only left it a few times. "A walk sounds like a good idea," she said, getting to her feet to follow him outside.

They walked along the beach near the tide line, which was easily discerned in the moonlight. Travis lighted a cheroot and the aroma was sweet and pleasant. The endless rhythm of the waves crashing and receding calmed her as the cool night breeze caressed her skin. Walking beside him, Susan sighed with a surprising contentment and gazed out at the sea, dark and mysterious with the moon's reflection shimmering like a distant puddle of liquid silver.

Travis glanced over at her. "Makes you feel insignificant, doesn't it? All that power—the sheer inexorability of it."

"It's peaceful now," Susan murmured. "It almost seems kind, but I know it can be terrifying during a hurricane. Have you ever been in one?"

"Not a really destructive one, like the one in the 1800's that leveled St. John's church. Other islands have suffered in this century more than we. They've experienced volcanic eruptions, too —like the one that killed my parents."

Susan looked up at him in surprise. It was the first time he had mentioned his parents to her, except for that once in Miami when he had said his mother had walked out on him when he was ten. It was too dark to see his expression clearly, although the angles of his profile stood out more darkly than the surrounding night. "I never knew how your parents died," she said. "How old were you?"

"Ten."

The same age as when his mother left. Had his father deserted him, too? "I'm sorry," she murmured. "I—I know it was a long time ago, but it must have affected you, losing both your parents at such an early age."

"I'm sure it did, although I'm not fully aware of the ways in which I might have been different if they hadn't died. I doubt that the difference would be as great as you think. I never felt really close to either of them. They seemed not to need other people, only each other. I guess I felt left out."

"They must have loved each other very much."

He shrugged. "I'm not sure if it was love or hate—a mixture more likely. I have clearer memories of their fighting than of anything else. We came to live at the plantation when I was seven, and my mother hated it. She always wanted to go back to England, and they argued about that a lot. I heard them at night after I'd gone to bed."

Susan had a fleeting picture of Travis as a young child, huddled alone in his bed, listening to his parents arguing, frightened by it and perhaps crying. The imagined scene stirred her compassion. "Why did they stay, if they were so unhappy here?"

"I didn't know at the time. Later, I realized that my father was too weak to defy my grandfather. Harris would have cut him off without a cent if he had left. Here, our material needs were taken care of; my father didn't have to provide for our support. I doubt that he could have. He was simply a man who wanted to be left alone to idle away his life in peace. He might even have been content here if my mother hadn't kept at him all the time."

"How did they come to be on another island when the volcano erupted?"

He made an ironic sound and threw down the stub of his cheroot, stopping to crush it under his shoe heel. They continued walking. "My mother finally reached her breaking point and bolted. But she had very little money and only made it as far as a neighboring island. Then she phoned my father and told him to meet her and bring whatever money he could pry out of my grandfather. I assume she wanted him to go back to England with her. Perhaps she thought if they left me with Harris, he would let them go."

A rush of sympathy went through her. What awful knowledge for a ten-year-old boy to deal with. His mother hadn't even cared enough to take him with her when she left. She'd been willing to trade him for her freedom, and apparently she had expected her husband to feel no more concern for their son than she did. Perhaps he hadn't.

"And your father did as she asked."

"Not exactly. When he went to my grandfather for money, Harris refused. Instead, he told him to be a man for once and go and collect his wife and bring her back home. Harris didn't suffer fools gladly." There was the same bitter edge to his words as she had heard when he had first mentioned his mother.

"You respected him a great deal, didn't you?"

"Harris? Yes. Oh, not for a long time—years. After my parents were killed I decided that he was to blame for every unhappy thing that had ever befallen me—my parents' arguing, my mother's running away and leaving me behind, even the volcanic eruption that took their lives. Children have a simple black-and-white way of looking at things. When I went away to college, I never meant to come back here or see my grandfather again. But, he became seriously ill—"

"When he needed you, you couldn't turn your back on him?"

"Something like that. Anyway, I came back and took over the plantation and the bank. I even came to care for him quite a lot before he died. I think he knew it, although I never told him so. It would have embarrassed him too much. And I didn't want him to think I was trying to ingratiate myself." He grunted. "As it turned out, perhaps I should have."

She knew that he was thinking about the provisions of the inheritance and, also, that he was too proud ever to have uttered a word to his grandfather, even if he'd known about the will. "You resent him for the will, don't you?"

"Some," he admitted. "Once I'd calmed down, I realized that Harris thought it was in my best interests. He always thought he knew what was best for everyone, even when they didn't know it themselves. I think he was afraid I'd wait too long to marry and die without a son to take over the plantation. He couldn't stand the thought of its going out of the family. So he decided to give me a push." He was watching her. "As things have fallen out, I think he did me a favor."

She disliked the trend the conversation was taking and refused to rise to that last remark. They walked along without speaking for some time. Finally, she said, "I guess we do have to grow up before we can accept the fact that those we care about are both good and bad, like all other people. Your grandfather evidently had a strong sense of family loyalty and responsibility, but he had little patience with those who opposed him." She wondered if Travis realized that the same could be said of him.

"That's as accurate an assessment as any," he said carelessly. "I wonder, though, why you can't forgive *my* mistakes if you really think that everyone is both good and bad."

"What you did was a little more than a mistake."

He was silent, as if he were thinking about what she had said. Then, minutes later, he spoke. "Let's rest here a bit before we go back." He steered her a short distance away from the beach where a smooth grassy patch of ground ran down to meet the sand. He sat on the grass and, after only a moment's hesitation, she sank down beside him, leaving a space between them.

The breeze seemed to have picked up and, now that they were no longer moving, Susan began to feel chilled. She shivered, hugging herself, and ran her hands along her arms. She wanted to go back and had turned to Travis to suggest it when she felt his fingers at her nape, pushing under the heavy silken fall of her hair. For a long moment, she couldn't speak as her heart drummed in her ears. Then his fingers moved from her neck to trace an invisible line across her bare shoulder and down the quivering length of her arm.

"You're shivering. Are you cold?"

Susan moved away from him and drew a steadying breath. "Yes; I'd like to go back to the cottage."

"Is that really what you'd like? Or is there a part of you that wants to stay here with me?"

"No—no, I have to go now or—"

"Or you might give in to what you really want." It was not a question. He captured her hand and was stroking the palm with the tip of his tongue.

"Oh, Travis—" The gasped words were desperate as she tried to drag her hand from his grasp. "You shouldn't . . ."

"But I should." He lifted his head and his face was so near to her that she could clearly make out all his features. Her pulses raced at the raw desire she knew was in his eyes. "I have to—or go crazy."

Then his mouth descended and she thought, almost fatalistically, that it was like the moment before a driver crashes into something, the moment when he realizes what's coming and all his senses leap into life and he tries frantically to keep his head. Her hands splayed out against his chest in an effort to force some distance between them, but his tongue was parting her lips with little effort. The urgency of his mouth had a mesmerizing sweetness. She felt herself sinking back against the soft grass, his weight pressing her down, the drugging intoxication of his kiss silencing her protests. For so long she had denied all the good thoughts of him, had kept all the happy times at bay and cultivated her anger and resentment, but now all that was real was his nearness, his body touching hers, and the trembling response of her senses.

"Susan," he groaned, his mouth moving to the tender skin beneath her earlobe, while his hand slid down to push at the knit material covering her. Urgently, he freed the ripe fullness of her breasts from the binding fabric. "So lovely," he murmured, his tongue finding one thrusting tip and caressing it tenderly.

"Travis." His name had the weak, hopeless sound of a dying appeal.

"I'm going mad wanting you," he muttered huskily. "Don't keep fighting me. . . ."

She was devastated by her own increasing awareness of the feel of his lean body over hers, his hardening demand, and a part of her delighted in the knowledge that she could arouse him in spite of the fact that he didn't love her.

Her breasts had grown tender with her pregnancy and, while his seeking mouth was driving her senses wild, she was also aware of discomfort. Perhaps it was the hint of pain that edged her back toward sense. How could she lie there compliantly and allow him to use her like this—again? She began trying to wriggle away from him.

But when his mouth sought hers again, reason was stifled. Whether it was the isolation of the beach and the darkness that shut them in, as if they were the only human beings in the universe, or the fact that he hadn't touched her for so long, she didn't know. But she was aware of her hands reaching up for him, tangling in his thick dark hair and pulling him closer. Only this one moment was real. She hadn't fully realized before how utterly wanton her emotions could make her or the depth of the longing he was capable of stirring in her. She was wracked by a desperate hunger for which there could be only one satisfaction.

Her hands slid from his hair, creeping inside the neck of his shirt so that his hair-roughened chest rubbed against her palms.

"Thank God!" he muttered shakily, raking back her falling hair with unsteady hands. "I was so afraid that you didn't want me now, but you do—you do. I know that I've hurt you, but you still belong to me."

The conviction and triumph in the words made her freeze. That was all she had ever been to him, a possession, a vessel to carry and nourish his heir. She tugged at the knit fabric of her top, covering her breasts with trembling fingers. "I don't belong to you," she said, unable to disguise the tremor in her voice. "I—I belong only to myself."

His body had become a dead weight on hers as he stared down into her face. "What are you trying to do to me?"

"Aren't you confused? It's what *you* are trying to do to *me*. Well, I'm not strong enough to stop you. I know that. But I'll hate every minute of it. So, if you still want me, knowing that—"

"Stop it!" he interrupted her harshly. "I'm not an animal. I've never forced a woman in my life."

Susan ran her tongue over lips that were swollen from his plundering kisses. "Let me go."

He rolled off her, coming to a sitting position, his fists clenched on his knees. "Go then!" His voice was thick with disgust. "Go back and hide in the cottage."

With controlled movements, Susan sat up, then got to her feet. She was shaking, very near tears, as the knowledge sank in that she had come within a hair of letting him make love to her. She had wanted him wildly, still wanted him, even as she shook with a feeling of reprieve. Somehow, at the last moment, she had managed to grasp the remnant of her pride. She must not allow him to dominate her in this way as in all others.

For one brief moment she almost wished she had not learned about the will. Ignorance *could* be bliss. She knew that his physical need for her was real, but she also knew that his greatest need was to make her pregnant. He had even told her as much on their wedding day. How much she had wanted his children then! And he had assured her that he felt the same way. She could still hear the caress in his voice. "I want *your* children . . . the sooner the better . . . I want to watch them grow up." Lies, all of it. Oh, he had to have a child, but hers would be no more precious to him than Kay Harte's or some other suitable woman's. It was merely that she had been the easiest to deceive. She wondered desperately how much longer she could keep from him the knowledge that she was already carrying his child.

The incident, and the conversation that had preceded it, remained with Susan long after she had reached the cottage and shut herself in her bedroom, where she lay listening to the steady rise and fall of the tide beyond the enclosing walls. She wanted to feel nothing for Travis, she told herself—not sympathy, least of all love. The irrational wish that she was experiencing in these long night hours to understand him better was ridiculous—and dangerous. Pity was an emotion she could not afford, unless it was for herself.

The sadness of the story he had told her seemed etched into her mind. She could not stop thinking of it, of the lonely child Travis must have been. Travis of the British Sennetts, who had settled on Barbados before 1700, put down deep roots there, and become important in that small, confining world. He had labeled his parents fools, said that he could not even remember what his mother looked like. But she had heard the jagged edge of pain in the words. Did the scars caused by his foolish, selfish parents go so deep?

The next day the strain between them was back as strong as ever. Neither of them mentioned what had happened on the beach, but it was between them as they sat at breakfast, trying to make idle conversation. Susan was vastly relieved when, immediately after breakfast, he left the cottage to drive to a lagoon some distance farther north for snorkeling, saying curtly that he would not be back for lunch.

As it turned out, he didn't return for dinner either, and she had to throw away most of a casserole and a melon salad. She had gone to bed when she heard him come in, his steps slow and unsteady. He had been drinking. She clutched a pillow against her face when she heard his footsteps pause outside her door, and released her held breath when, after a long moment, the steps moved away again and she heard the opening and closing of the other bedroom door.

They returned to the plantation the next afternoon. Travis had emerged from his bedroom at noon to rummage through a cabinet for the aspirin bottle. She did not comment on the reason for his headache, nor did he. In fact, he said very little as he picked at the lunch she had prepared, announcing when he had finished that they would leave as soon as she could be ready.

When they arrived at the plantation, Travis changed clothes and left to see his overseer. Assailed by the restlessness that she had kept under control while they were at the cottage, Susan went into the study and began sorting through the papers in the desk. She soon saw that Travis had not exaggerated the disorder his records were in. At first she had a few reservations about what she was doing. Would Travis interpret it as evidence of an interest in the plantation and its workings? Would he see it as proof that she had accepted the marriage as inevitable, perhaps even desirable?

The reservations were easily overcome, however, by the prospect of having something useful to do with her time. More than an hour later, she had emptied three of the desk drawers and had stacked the contents in five piles on the desk top in the rudimentary beginnings of a filing system.

She was looking into the empty four-drawer file cabinet for folders when Mala entered the room.

"Miz Susan, you got a caller."

Susan looked up absentmindedly. "Who is it?"

"Only me." Violet, who had followed Mala to the study, now stepped inside. She eyed the cluttered desk. "Goodness, what's all this?"

Susan closed the file drawer. "I'm working out a filing system for Travis. How are you, Violet?" She was surprised that the cousins were still on Barbados. What did they hope to accomplish here? It would be more than a year before anything could be finally settled. Did they intend to stay until then? Violet was wearing a gaudy pantsuit, its color seeming to emphasize the freckles on her arms. Someone ought to tell her, Susan thought, that hot pink isn't her color.

Her inclination was to get rid of the woman as quickly as possible. She recalled Travis's warning her not to talk to his cousins because they were troublemakers. That, of course, was when he thought he could keep her from discovering why he had married her. Now the memory of his words made her feel obstinate, and she forced herself to be pleasant. "You couldn't have come at a better time. I could use a break. Mala, would you bring us something cold to drink? Iced tea would be nice."

It was clear that Mala didn't like the idea of leaving Susan and Violet alone. Probably Travis had suggested that she keep an eye on his cousins whenever they were in the house. But in the face of a direct request from Travis's wife, she would comply, though not cheerfully. She frowned at Violet's back before she muttered a low "Yes'm" and left.

"Sit down, Violet." Susan indicated a chair and flopped down on the leather couch.

"You've been away," Violet said.

"How did you know?"

"I called you the day before yesterday. I thought you might like to meet me in town for lunch." She glanced toward the door with a dark look. "That awful Mala was positively rude. She refused to tell me where you were or when you'd be back. All she would say was that you and Travis were away on vacation. Honestly, that woman has no conception of her proper place. I'd fire her so fast she wouldn't know what hit her."

Susan chuckled, imagining Mala's stubborn refusal to satisfy Violet's curiosity. "Mala's been here so long, she considers herself a member of the family. She does have a tendency to bully us, but she's fiercely loyal. That's quite a point in her favor."

Violet grimaced. "The old family retainer, eh?" She was studying Susan intently. "If I were you, I'd let Mala know who's boss from the beginning."

"That's the problem, I think. She already knows." Susan laughed. "Actually, Mala and I get along very well." The servants were the least of her worries. It was Travis who was causing all of her problems. "I'm a little surprised that you and Curt are still here."

"You mean because Travis has been so hateful to us?" She snorted. "We're used to his nasty moods. He's the spitting image of our grandfather. Besides, we have a number of acquaintances in Bridgetown. They've been far more gracious than Travis, so I imagine we'll stay around for a few more weeks, at least, as long as we're already here. It's the first vacation we've had in some time." She ran brightly painted fingernails through her thick, red hair, a nervous gesture. In fact, almost everything about Violet suggested nervousness—the way she repeatedly fingered the scooped neck of her tunic, the way one crossed leg swung back and forth in a jerking motion, making her backless sandal flop against her heel, the slightly harried look in her green eyes. She was a high-strung woman whose unsettled nature seemed barely restrained.

Mala appeared with the tea tray, which she set on the table between the two women and then, after a slanting look of disapproval for Violet, she went out again.

"This is a perfect example of Mala's impudence," Violet complained, picking up her glass. "She didn't even bring lemon slices, and she knows I prefer my tea with lemon."

"We're probably out of lemon," Susan said. "I

think I heard that there's a shortage of citrus fruit in the areas that supply the island."

Violet grunted her disbelief, sure that Mala was being deliberately impertinent. Then she said, "Tell me, where did you go for your vacation?"

"St. John's Parish. We borrowed a beach cottage."

Violet gazed at her. "How romantic."

Avoiding the woman's avidly inquisitive look, Susan responded, "It was relaxing."

Violet's green eyes ran over her in a way that made Susan feel uncomfortable. "Well, it appears that you've fallen completely under Travis's spell."

What did she mean by that? Violet's expression held a touch of scorn now, as if she knew something demeaning about Susan. She couldn't possibly have guessed that Susan was pregnant. Or could she? Susan had always heard that pregnant women have a certain "look," even in the first months. Maybe Violet *had* noticed a change in her. She decided that the best course was to pretend to be unaware of the scornful undertone in Violet's remark. The woman had made an art of innuendo; it was quite possible that she suspected nothing but had learned that mysterious statements sometimes evoked information from others.

"The vacation was a mutual decision. We both needed a change of scene."

"I must say, you don't look particularly robust, and now he's got you doing his secretarial work."

"Don't be absurd, Violet. I like having something to do. I've discovered it's a bit boring, being a lady of leisure."

Violet made a sarcastic sound. "Can't you find something more interesting than filing? You must get out more, make new friends. At least you've made one—and you couldn't have chosen better. Jonathan Wicksham is a charmer, isn't he?"

Susan set down her glass and rested her elbow on the couch arm, supporting her head with her hand. "I thought you mistrusted all men."

"That doesn't keep me from noticing the attractive ones."

"I didn't know you knew Jonathan."

"I don't know him very well. Curt and I ran into him in a restaurant the other day and Curt introduced me. He was alone, so we had lunch with him."

"And Jonathan mentioned that he and I were friends? How did that come about?"

"He knew of our relationship to Travis, so it was only natural. He said he'd given a dinner party for you and Travis, and that he'd been showing you some of the sights of the island."

"Yes, he has." Susan was getting the impression that the conversation was making Violet uneasy. Maybe she was embarrassed at having admitted to discussing Susan with a stranger. "He's been very kind to me."

Violet set her glass down abruptly. "Listen, I won't keep you from your dreary occupation any longer. I just wanted to say hello and ask if you'd like to have lunch before I leave."

Susan hesitated, not willing to be unnecessarily cruel. "I'll have to see when I'm free. This filing is going to keep me busy for a while. I'll call you when I can find a convenient time."

Violet got to her feet. "Fine." After a moment, she added, "There's no reason why you and I can't be friends, regardless of what disagreements I might have with Travis."

Susan was no more inclined to trust Violet's "friendship" than she had been the first time they talked. She sensed that everything the woman did had some hidden motive, and family intrigue did not appeal to her. "Thanks for coming by," she said, her tone forestalling any more conversation. "Now I really must get back to work."

After Violet had gone, she took a package of folders from the file cabinet and began to label them. Some moments later, she paused, her attention diverted by the sudden memory of something Violet had said. Curt had introduced Violet to Jonathan. If that was what had really happened—and who could ever be sure that what Violet said was strictly true?—when had *Curt* met Jonathan? She was almost certain that Jonathan had told her he didn't know Travis's cousins.

He must have met Curt soon after telling her that. Then she recalled Violet mentioning acquaintances in Bridgetown. One of them must have introduced Curt and Jonathan. It was of no significance, at any rate, except that she always felt she had to be on guard with Violet, suspicious of everything she said or did.

She shrugged these distracting thoughts aside and went back to the task at hand.

Chapter Ten

Working on the filing system made the days pass more quickly for Susan. Sometime after they had returned from the beach cottage she had all of Travis's records and loose papers filed in neatly labeled folders that filled two drawers of the cabinet. The only problem was that when he wanted to find anything now, she could lay hands on it much faster than he could. After a couple of frustrating attempts to locate a particular record, he began to ask her for what he wanted without even looking for it himself.

It wasn't that she minded particularly. In fact, it was the only way to keep the filing system in order. But she was nagged by the feeling that she was becoming more and more enmeshed in Travis's life. Further, she suspected she was using the office work to put off thinking about her situation and what she ought to do about it; and the day was fast approaching when her pregnancy would be apparent for all to see. Now in the end of her fifth month, she had taken to wearing loose fitting shirts with her shorts and slacks. She continued to feel chronically tired, too, but now she could blame that on the long hours of office work. Travis began to urge her to be less conscientious, saying, "I never meant to turn you into a drudge."

Jonathan had phoned her several times since her holiday with invitations for dinner, and each time she had begged off. The truth was that she regretted having confided so completely in him, good friend though he was. If she hadn't been at such a low emotional point at the time, she would never have done it. But now she began to worry that he might have interpreted the confidences concerning her marriage as a hint that she could be interested in him as more than a friend—if not now, perhaps after the baby was born.

She didn't realize that he would take her refusals to see him as an attempt to dissolve their friendship altogether until Jonathan called at the house to see her. He looked anxious when Mala showed him into the sunny, wicker-furnished sitting room where Susan was relaxing after a morning spent at work in the study.

"Jonathan! What a nice surprise." She laid aside her magazine and extended her hand. He took it, squeezing gently, before he sat down on the couch next to her.

"Thank you for the warm welcome."

"Did you really expect any other kind?"

"Frankly, yes." He looked apologetic.

"How can you say that, Jonathan? You know I treasure your friendship."

"I know that you did at one time. Lately you've turned down my invitations and I was afraid you'd changed your mind—or that you were sorry for saying some of the things you said at our last meeting."

Susan looked at her hands clasped in her lap. "You know me too well." She glanced up with a smile. "I *have* wished that I hadn't run on so that evening, though probably not for the reasons you think. I've never liked women who go around telling their troubles to anyone who will listen. It's in such poor taste."

He looked relieved. "My dear Susan, you didn't tell your troubles to just anyone. I'm your friend, and I hope you haven't been upsetting yourself with the thought that I've repeated a syllable of what you said to anyone."

She shook her head. "No. I think I can trust you to keep your word."

His expression was solemn. "You can, you know. Have you told Travis?"

"Not yet." She felt suddenly restless and got up to walk to a window, where she stood looking out for a moment. Then she turned to him. "I'll be forced to soon, but I want to have some things worked out in my mind first."

"My offer of help is still open. I'll do anything I can to make this easier for you."

She wondered if he was referring to the abortion they had discussed previously. But the time for that alternative had run out and, besides, her feelings on that score hadn't changed. In fact, the longer she carried the child, the more unacceptable thoughts of an abortion had become. In truth, she had started to wonder what the baby would look like, to want it. Most of the time she managed to disassociate it from Travis and think of the child as hers alone.

"It's a comfort to know that you're available if I need you," she said, "but this is my problem and I'll have to deal with it."

His silver-gray eyes looked bleak for a moment. "You seem less strained, at any rate. Your vacation with your husband must have agreed with you."

"It was restful, although I didn't expect it to be." She frowned. "How did you know we'd been away? Did you telephone while I was gone?"

"As a matter of fact, Travis's cousin, Curt Winston, told me. We met through a mutual acquaintance, and I've seen him a few times since."

"Yes, Violet said you'd lunched together."

He raised an eyebrow. "You've seen Violet? I was under the impression that the two branches of the family hardly spoke."

"I'm trying to keep out of family squabbles. Violet came by to see me after we'd returned from our vacation."

"Then you know she's returned to England."

"No, I didn't." Susan experienced a small pang of guilt because she hadn't followed through with her promise to call Violet about lunch. But at the same time she was glad that the matter had been taken out of her hands. "I expect they were getting bored. When did they go?"

"Violet left yesterday. Curt's still at the hotel in Bridgetown. He's interested in making some investments in the Caribbean, and I've promised to advise him. We may become partners in a small enterprise."

Apparently Curt and Jonathan had seen quite a lot of each other in recent weeks. It was understandable, of course, that Curt would seek Jonathan's advice. From what Travis had said, Jonathan was quite shrewd in business matters. And Curt and Violet did have their inheritance from their grandfather. Curt probably wanted to put it into something where the potential for profit was greater than in stocks and bonds. Perhaps the cousins had more financial sense than Travis gave them credit for. Certainly they couldn't have picked a better adviser than Jonathan.

"It's considerate of you to help Curt."

He laughed. "Consideration has little to do with it. I wouldn't put money into anything that I didn't think was a sound investment. But there are circumstances when it's wise to have partners to share the risk. Curt Winston has money to invest and I think we'll deal together well enough, particularly since I'll retain a controlling interest."

"I don't know much about investing, I'm afraid. You may not believe it, but it seems rather boring to me."

His cool eyes ran over her appreciatively. "No more talk of business then. Beautiful women should never have to think about money."

It occurred to Susan that Mala and Amii might be speculating about what she and Jonathan were doing so long in the sitting room alone. She had seen Mala's suspicious glance at him as she'd shown him in. She decided it might be wiser to continue their visit in less privacy.

On the veranda the maids could see them from the back windows, and they would be in full view of the gardener or any of the field workers who happened by. "Why don't we go out to the veranda? I'll ask Mala to bring us something cold to drink."

Jonathan stayed for the better part of an hour, so long that Susan began to feel uneasy about the prospect of Travis returning to the house and making a scene. Mala would probably tell him about Susan's caller, anyway, but Susan preferred that Jonathan not be present when Travis heard of it. He had made it abundantly clear that he didn't approve of her spending time with the man, and she had little doubt that he would say the same to Jonathan.

But finally Jonathan rose to leave and she saw him out of the house, grateful that nothing had occurred to disrupt the tranquility of the visit. She promised to meet him for lunch soon and shut the door before she wiped the dampness off her face with the back of her hand. It had been extremely warm on the veranda. She decided to relax in a tepid bath.

Upstairs, she poured a generous amount of bath crystals into the large, sunken tub and undressed as the rushing water rose, creating great mounds of white bubbles.

She sank into the gardenia-scented water with a long, rapturous sigh, lowering herself until the bubbles covered her to her shoulders and her head rested against the slanted end of the tub. Heavenly, she decided, closing her eyes and relaxing until she felt weightless.

She was drifting into sleep when she was

jerked back to alertness by the sound of a door opening and heavy footsteps crossing her bedroom. Then the bathroom door flew open and Travis stood there in his work clothes, his legs in tall, dusty boots spread almost the width of the door.

His eyes, dark with anger, surveyed her. Susan started into a sitting position at the sight of him, then realized that she had almost exposed herself and sank lower in the water. A flush warmed her cheeks. "How dare you barge in here without knocking!"

"Oh, no you don't!" he grated, walking farther into the bathroom. "I won't be put on the defensive. What was Wicksham doing in this house?"

So, one of the servants had told him already. She looked up at him resentfully, feeling like a prisoner in the tub since she couldn't get away without parading into the bedroom naked. "It was a social call. Surely your spies told you all about it. We were on the veranda, in plain sight."

"I've told you before, I won't have him here. What did he want?"

"You should have had Mala tape our conversation!" she flared. "I said it was a social call, and that's all I'm going to say. I don't have to explain myself or my friends to you!"

"Is that a fact?" His voice was too soft suddenly, and she darted a suspicious look at him. He was standing beside the tub now, looking straight down at her, and she didn't like what she saw in his eyes. His gaze never left her face as his hands began to strip off his shirt.

"Wh–what are you doing? You can't—"

He bent and tugged off his boots, one after the other, and then his socks, still looking at her with that dangerous fire in his eyes. He jerked at his belt buckle, unfastening it.

Her stunned mind finally comprehended what he intended. She hesitated another moment. The dilemma over whether to stay and be joined by her husband or step out of the tub, exposing herself fully, was too much for her. In that moment of hesitation, he stepped out of his jeans, rid himself of his briefs and climbed into the tub.

Left with no other choice, she rose from the water. "Enjoy your bath. I'm leaving." She made herself meet his bold gaze haughtily and tried to step out. But her attempt at bravado was futile. He caught her around the waist and hauled her against him.

"You're not going anywhere."

She was pulled back down into the water with him until, mercifully, her nakedness was once more obscured by bubbles. But now his body was stretched beside hers, touching her along the full length of one side. He traced the curve of her cheek and jaw with warm, hard fingers that then trailed down her throat and roamed over her body beneath the water. The bubble bath made their skin slippery and his hand slid over her like satin against satin. She felt overwhelmed by weakness as the pleasure of his caress invaded her senses.

She made a feeble attempt to move away from him. "No—don't—" The words were the merest suggestion of a breathless whisper.

Almost reverently, his eyes roamed over her

flushed face. Slowly his fingers explored the outline of one breast, moving with delightful tenderness toward the tip.

"Don't waste your breath," he said softly, his warm breath fanning her lips as his mouth descended with maddening slowness. "I'm listening to your body this time instead of to your words, and your body is enjoying this immensely." His fingers had encircled the thrusting tautness that proved the truth of what he said and, as he continued to stroke, the new tenderness pushed a gasp of mingled pleasure and pain from Susan.

His lips touched hers gently and set off a quivering response that made her return the kiss eagerly, moving her mouth sensuously against his. He lifted his head to look into her eyes, The anger over Jonathan's visit was gone; his face was filled with hunger, his eyelids heavy.

Susan could not protest, could only stare at him in trembling uncertainty. Her body arched involuntarily as his eager hand continued its meticulous exploration into the most secret parts of her body, evoking a wildfire of response wherever it touched. Her drowning brain cried that he was only using her, that he was conquering her without a fight, but her body yearned for the feel of him, the balm for her clamoring senses that only he could give.

His hand rested on her stomach and the sound of their mingled breathing was rapid and harsh in the somnolent afternoon silence.

Suddenly his hand grew still. He released her lips to look into her face. "Your body has changed. You've gained weight." Frowning, and with an almost clinical interest, he ran his hand over her breasts and across her stomach again. She saw the sudden flare deep in his eyes the instant understanding began to dawn. "You're pregnant!" His voice was roughened by emotion. "Aren't you? Answer me, Susan!"

She closed her eyes and groaned, knowing that it was useless to lie. "Yes," she whispered.

She felt a sudden tenseness in him. "Is Wicksham the father?"

Her eyes flew open in amazement. There was anger waiting in his expression. "Jonathan has never even kissed me! Besides, I'm almost six months along. The baby is yours, blast you! You're absolutely vile to doubt it! Now, please—" She looked away. "Please, let me out of here."

A laugh of pure triumph escaped him. He stood up, water and bubbles sliding down his magnificent male body, and stepped out of the tub. Bending, he scooped her into his arms and headed for the bedroom, water streaming from both of them onto the carpet.

He deposited her in the middle of the bed, swept her naked, glistening body with a masterful look and followed her down. Then, with all the considerable powers at his command, he began to arouse her anew with a deliberate, inexorable slowness. She closed her eyes weakly, tears clogging her throat. This could not be happening. She could not be uttering these little sighs of pleasure and pleading.

"Please, Travis, no," she whispered, but her ragged words ended with a betraying sigh.

His groan was a blend of conquest and yearning. "I couldn't stop now, even if I wanted to." The unsteady admission might have been an apology, but it sounded more like justification. He knelt beside her and cupped the weight of both breasts in his hands, his thumbs gently stroking. His low chuckle brimmed with desire. Then he bent so that his mouth could follow where his hands had been. She writhed helplessly.

"You want this as much as I do."

A weak sound of surrender escaped her. "Say it, Susan. Tell me that you want me. Please . . . I have to hear the words."

"I . . . want you." Then, as if the admission had finally broken her last restraint, she clung to him, pulling his hard body down over hers, entering the storm of their mingled passion with him eagerly until she was filled with a wild longing so strong that she thought she must be mad. Lost in the abandoned release of passion, she cried out his name.

Trembling, she surfaced from the dizzying pool of desire. Travis wrapped his arms around her, sighing heavily, and pulled her back against him, his cheek against her hair, his arm encircling her waist, their legs bent slightly and fitting together.

Too sated and drowsy even to think, Susan snuggled contentedly against him and drifted into sleep.

Late afternoon shadows were long when she came slowly back to wakefulness, confused until she recalled where she was and what had happened. Then self-loathing made her blush. How could she have been so weak? She turned her head and found that she was alone in the bed. Someone had pulled the thin cotton spread over her body. Travis?

She crept out of bed, as if she had no right there, and dressed in a loose, yellow cotton sundress. It was one of the few dresses she owned without a waistline and she had never particularly liked it before. She would have to buy some maternity clothes soon, she thought, and wondered if Kay Harte carried them. She had never believed herself capable of deliberate cruelty, but at the moment the idea of the woman who was carrying Travis's child buying maternity wear from the other woman who loved him appealed to her bitter mood. She discarded the thought that it would be striking out at Kay because she couldn't strike at Travis —and, also, that Kay could have been in Susan's place had she been willing to throw pride out the window.

Had Travis proposed to Kay first? Susan sank down in front of her dressing table and idly picked up her hair brush. Of course he had! He must know that Kay was in love with him. When he had learned about the will, it must have been the first thought to enter his mind. He'd had more respect for Kay than for Susan, apparently, for he'd told her about the will, probably believing that she loved him enough to marry him anyway. But she hadn't. Good for Kay. In other circumstances, she felt that she and Kay Harte could have become close friends.

She began to brush her hair, ashamed of her

spiteful desire to punish Kay for something that was none of her doing. Lord, was she going to become as selfish and cynical as Violet? Not if she could help it, and for starters she'd find somewhere other than Kay's Boutique to buy maternity clothes.

She heard the bedroom door opening quietly and turned to see Travis. He paused for a split second as his eyes flicked over the rumpled bed. When he saw that she was up, he walked in. He was dressed in cream-colored trousers and a cinnamon silk shirt, and his expression was so complacent that Susan itched to slap him. How dare he look so calm and pleased with himself! He was the one who should feel embarrassed and guilty, and it maddened her that *she* was the one who felt that way.

She turned back to the mirror and continued brushing her hair with more vigorous strokes than before. If she hadn't been so angry, she might have noticed the hesitancy in his stance as he came to a stop behind her or the hopeful look in his dark eyes or the tautness of his muscles. But she was too preoccupied with her own humiliation to see anything but his arrogance.

"Well, you missed a half day's work," she snapped. "No doubt you'll be able to make it up later."

Travis was looking at her face where it was reflected in the mirror, and the lines fanning out from his eyes deepened in an amused expression. "I was occupied with more enjoyable pursuits."

Subduing a recalcitrant wife, Susan thought.

She noticed how his thick black lashes had come down to screen his look, how the tanned skin of his face glowed with health and vitality, how his hair molded itself so attractively to his head. Furious, she repressed a desire to touch him. She would not be a self-effacing, humble female.

He placed a hand lightly on her shoulder. "I've missed you, darling. I can't tell you how happy you've made me this afternoon."

Of course she had! She'd told him she was carrying his child. Wasn't that the whole point of this marriage? "I think I have a vague idea. The baby means the inheritance is all yours—provided I don't miscarry."

A flash of concern drew his brows together. "There aren't any problems, are there?"

"Problems?" She uttered a brittle laugh. "Why, of course not, Travis. Everything is hunky dory. I haven't seen a doctor, but I assure you I'm disgustingly healthy."

"You should have seen a doctor by now. It's careless of you not to have done so. I'll have Mala make an appointment for you tomorrow."

His hand on her shoulder pressed warmly against her skin, making her aware of him in a way that she did not want to be. She shrugged it off and turned around on the vanity stool to look up at him. "I'll tell you why I haven't seen a doctor. At first, I tried to convince myself I wasn't pregnant. Since I can't do that any longer, I've been trying to decide what to do about it."

His eyes glinted with sudden anger. "If you mean what I think you mean . . ."

"Yes, Travis, I gave serious consideration to

an abortion." She was lying, but she wanted to hurt him and it was the only weapon at hand. "Unfortunately, I seem to have too many old-fashioned hangups for that. Now it's too late." She rose and started to walk away from him.

He grabbed her arm and whirled her about to face him. "If you had destroyed this child, I'd have made you regret it!"

"You couldn't have made me regret it any more than I'll regret having it," she said in a low voice. "If there was any other way out of it, believe me, I'd take it."

His dark eyes glittered, and then she felt his grip relax. "We have to stop cutting each other up like this, Susan. It can't be good for you or the baby. Thousands of marriages have worked with far less than we have going for us."

She twisted from his relaxed grip and walked across the room to stand behind a chair. The padded back gave her something to hang on to. "Do you think a good marriage can be built on sex alone? We're good in bed. So what? I'm sure you can—and do—find that with Kay—and others, for all I know. Don't think that just because you overcame my resistance this afternoon I'm willing to forgive and forget."

"This isn't the first time you've suggested that I'm having an affair with Kay Harte. It isn't true. She's never been more than a friend to me. As for overcoming your resistance," he added mockingly, "you were as eager as I was, and you know it. I could make you want me, even now." He took a step toward her, but she stopped him with a shrill warning.

"Don't do it, Travis!" Tears sprang into her

eyes and she looked away, fighting to gain control of herself. She had been a willing partner this afternoon. Even now, just the sight of him struck a responsive chord in her. But she wouldn't let him own her. "I won't give in to you again. Nothing has changed."

They faced each other for a long moment, resentment stretching between them. "What exactly do you mean by that?" he asked finally.

"I mean," she choked out, "that I hate this place and I'm living for the day when I can leave."

All of the yielding left his face and was replaced by hard resolve. "If you have any idea of taking my child away from here, forget it!"

She leaned against the chair and covered her face with her hands. "Leave me alone! You've gotten what you want from me, haven't you?"

She didn't look up again until he ground out, "I won't be home for dinner."

She lifted her face then and retorted with all the bitterness of her pent-up rage, "Yes, run to sweet, understanding Kay! I'm sure she'll sympathize and comfort you!"

"That's not a bad idea!" He slammed out of the room and she sat down and gave in to tears of mingled fury and desperation.

She despised him! And herself even more because, God help her, she still loved him. Would this torment never end? Was he really going to Kay, or had he been speaking the truth when he had denied having an affair with her? She told herself that it didn't matter either way. After a few moments, she choked off the seemingly unending flood of tears and made herself get ready for dinner. She had to get control of her emotions, she told herself. Travis was right. Such inner tumult couldn't be good for the baby.

Two days later, she kept the appointment Mala had made for her in Bridgetown with the Sennett family physician. Dr. Elliott was a small, balding man in his sixties whose calm, confident manner immediately won Susan's trust. He gave her a thorough examination, after scolding her for waiting so long for her initial visit. In his office, after the examination, he told her that her blood count was a little low, which no doubt accounted for the perpetual tiredness she had noticed. He prescribed iron and vitamin tablets and gave her a list of foods she should eat every day. Then he made another appointment for a date three weeks away.

Within a week, everyone who knew Travis seemed to have heard of her pregnancy. Almost every time she went into town someone who had been at Jonathan's dinner party stopped her with congratulations. She tried to accept all the kind words with some semblance of grace, telling herself that everyone meant well, but it was difficult. Jonathan, whom she met for lunch or an afternoon drive almost every week, helped by just being there when she needed to talk.

She found a maternity shop and bought an adequate wardrobe for the coming months, but she had little joy in the selection. In fact, she had little joy in anything, it seemed. She felt as if she had put her life on hold and was just marking time until the baby came. Although Travis joined her for dinner almost every evening and, occasionally, took her out for dinner in a restaurant or to a friend's house, he seemed to have accepted her statement that nothing had changed between them. He made no effort to share her bed as the weeks dragged by.

Even though the state of affairs was just as she had vowed she wanted it, she suffered from mixed reactions. As her body changed and became cumbersome, she told herself that Travis no longer found her attractive. She should be grateful for not having to fight him off anymore but, for some strange reason, she wasn't.

One afternoon, late in the seventh month of her pregnancy, she slipped away from the house to a private beach on the Sennett property. She had been walking a mile or two every day, as her doctor had advised, but walking seemed particularly unattractive that afternoon and she decided to exercise by swimming.

No one ever used the private beach except for Travis, so there was no danger of anyone seeing her in her maternity swimsuit. The designer had done everything possible to make the one-piece suit attractive and had tried to disguise the wearer's bulging stomach with a short overskirt in front that fell from beneath the breasts. But when a woman is seven months along, no swim wear ever made can completely disguise the fact.

When she reached the beach, she removed her loose, sleeveless coverup, dropped it on the sand with her beach towel and waded into the water. She stayed near the shore, never venturing out into water that was over her head, and swam for a short time. She soon began to tire, though, and stretched out on the towel on her back to sun herself.

This was the position in which Travis found her awhile later. He came upon her without warning and was spreading his own beach towel beside hers when she realized she was not alone and her eyes flew open. She sat up abruptly. "I thought you had a meeting at the bank this afternoon."

"It was over a half hour ago. When I got back to the house, Mala told me where you'd gone." He was sitting with his knees drawn up, his arms resting carelessly on them. His skin looked as dark as copper in contrast to the pale beige swim trunks he wore. "I don't think it's a good idea for you to swim alone, especially in your condition."

She reached for her coverup, slipping it on over her suit and pulling the front edges together over her stomach. "I didn't go out far, and I stopped as soon as I began to feel tired. I won't do anything foolish."

His eyes, shot through with gold in the sunlight, raked over her. "There's always the danger of a cramp. If you'll let me know when you want to come swimming, I'll arrange things so I can come with you."

The solicitous manner that he had adopted toward her since he'd learned of her pregnancy made her feel self-conscious. Somehow she resented it. She gazed out over the water and wondered what she *did* want from him. Would she prefer that he ignore her condition, treat her unkindly? No, not that. In her mind a small voice taunted, *You want him to treat you like a woman again, admit it. You want him back in your bed.*

Perhaps a trace of the treacherous admission showed in her face, for Travis suddenly reached out and brushed the damp hairs away from her forehead with incredible tenderness. Then he bent to kiss her temple gently. "I care about what happens to you, Susan," he murmured softly. "It isn't only the baby."

Self-pitying tears tightened her throat. Lord, she was turning into a pathetic, weepy woman, and she had always hated them. "I—I'm fine. Dr. Elliott says so." She shifted away from him.

"Is my touch so repulsive to you?" That she had offended him was evident in the tightness of his tone. Well, she couldn't help it. She was too busy holding herself together to worry about his hurt feelings.

She darted a quick glance at him. "I don't want your pity, Travis. You don't have to pretend that you find me attractive. I know how clumsy and ugly I am now."

He laughed suddenly and pulled her head down on his shoulder. "Idiot! Don't you know that the woman who's carrying a man's child is always beautiful to him?"

Susan felt as though she would burst into tears any minute at his unexpected kindness. He *did* feel sorry for her. And, as usual, his thoughts were on the baby. She couldn't bear it, and she scrambled to her feet, snatching up her towel. "I've had enough sun; I'm going back to the house. See you at dinner."

If he replied, she didn't hear him as she

walked away. She had mastered the desire to weep by the time she reached the house. But a deep unhappiness remained as she bathed and dressed for dinner.

What was she going to do after the baby was born? The day would soon be upon her when she could no longer put off making a decision. She thought that Travis would let her go, provided she left the baby behind. Could she do that? Could she stand the thought of some other woman—Mala, or a second wife for Travis—caring for her child, loving it, giving it the things a mother should give? What would the baby think of her as he grew up? Wouldn't he, like Travis, think that his mother had traded him for her freedom? Inevitably, he would come to hate her.

She sighed helplessly. She didn't think she would be able to leave the baby, anyway. She would have to take him and run away. But, deep down, she knew that Travis would not rest until he had found them and brought the child back to Barbados.

Dear God, it was an impossible dilemma. Once again, she could not make a decision and she buried the distressing thoughts. She still had time before she had to decide.

Chapter Eleven

Christmas came and went with a depressing similarity to all the days before it. They had a tree and exchanged gifts, but Susan, in the final weeks of her pregnancy, refused almost all social invitations, of which there were many during the holiday season.

She had always thought that a tropical climate must be the next best thing to heaven. On Christmas Day the temperature was in the 80's, just as it had been in the spring when she'd come to the plantation as Travis's wife, and she realized that she was beginning to find the "heavenly" climate a little monotonous.

How she would have welcomed a heavy snowfall, she told herself, smiling at the impossibility of it. Anyway, it probably wasn't the climate at all that was making her feel so blue. It was her physical discomfort. Little aches seemed to assail every part of her body, her back and legs particularly. Although she had gained only fifteen pounds, it was all in front, and she felt huge and unbalanced. On her most recent visit to the doctor she had asked worriedly if he had detected more than one heartbeat. Dr. Elliott had laughed and assured her, "No, Susan. You're going to have only one baby. Take my word for it."

One morning late in January Jonathan phoned to ask if she felt like having lunch with him in Bridgetown. The prospect of getting out of the house for an hour or two was strongly appealing, and she agreed.

She pinned her hair atop her head and wore a white tent dress with low-heeled sandals. She'd given up high heels weeks ago when her feet had developed a tendency to swell.

When Jonathan handed her into his car, he said, "You look lovely, as usual, my dear."

Susan settled against the seat, trying to catch her breath, and laughed. "What a charming liar you are, Jonathan! Bless you, you've made me feel better already."

In deference to her condition, he took her to a secluded restaurant on the outskirts of Bridgetown. Since eating almost anything made Susan feel stuffed these days, she ordered a small chef's salad. They were having a cup of coffee to finish the meal when Curt Winston appeared in the doorway of the restaurant, squinting from having come into the dimness from the bright sunlight. After a moment, his eyes fell on Susan and Jonathan, and he smiled and walked over to their table.

"What a pleasant surprise, running into the two of you. Susan, you're looking well." The men shook hands. "I've tried to phone you at your office several times lately, Jonathan. I wanted us to get together for a talk."

"I've neglected business since before Christmas, I'm afraid," Jonathan told him. "Sit down, Curt." He glanced at Susan. "You don't mind, do you?"

She shook her head, wondering why Curt was still in town when Violet had gone. She hadn't seen or heard of him in weeks. Evidently his business with Jonathan was not yet settled.

"Why have you been trying to reach me?" Jonathan asked.

Curt darted an apologetic look at Susan. "I don't want to bore Susan by talking business."

"It's all right," she assured him. "In fact, if you gentlemen will excuse me, I'll be back in a few minutes." She retired to the ladies' room.

When she returned to the table, Curt was finishing a club sandwich as Jonathan talked earnestly. Looking up, Jonathan smiled. "Ah, here she is. Curt wants me to look at a piece of land that's for sale about five miles from here. I thought you might enjoy driving out there with us."

She thought of spending the long afternoon alone at the plantation and agreed. Curt, in the front seat with Jonathan's driver, half-turned so that he and Jonathan could continue their conversation. It seemed that Curt thought the piece of land would be a good site for some small tourist cabins and wanted Jonathan's opinion. "I've done some research," Curt was saying, "and learned that the number of tourists visiting the island has increased markedly in the last five years. The greatest need in accommodations is in the moderate price range—places where families with children can afford to stay for a week, perhaps cooking some of their own meals. An adequate kitchenette could be installed in each cabin using very little space."

As Curt continued to outline his ideas for eight or ten cabins, Susan laid her head back against the seat and closed her eyes, enjoying the air conditioning and the smooth movement of the Rolls.

A few minutes later, Curt was saying, "Stop here. It's about a quarter-mile down this lane. There's a good sea view."

The car halted and Susan lifted her head as Jonathan opened the door. "You'll probably enjoy stretching your legs, Susan." He helped her from the car and the three of them walked up a small incline as Curt pointed out the boundaries of the land that was for sale.

"I think we could save most of the trees. It would make the cabins seem more private, even though there would be only a few yards separating them. You can do a lot with shrubbery, too—and over there would be a good location for a swimming pool."

The path along which they were walking was rocky and Susan placed her feet carefully. Her balance wasn't as sure as it had been. She halted atop the little knoll to look across a narrow strip of weedy grass and down to where foamy white waves crashed against the rocky coast. Jonathan and Curt were behind her, deep in conversation about the cabins. From the corner of her eye, she saw Curt's arm gesturing widely to emphasize a point, and then there was the scrambling sound of shoes trying to gain a purchase on the loose rocks.

A weight hit Susan from behind and she was sliding, then falling down the incline. In a sheer reflex action, her hands grabbed onto clumps of weeds.

It all happened so quickly that she hadn't time to be afraid until she lay, unmoving, on her side, clutching at the weeds that had saved her from tumbling all the way to the edge of the cliff and over onto the rocks below.

Then she began to shake uncontrollably. She was aware of Jonathan and Curt scrambling down the incline to where she lay.

"Susan!" It was Jonathan's voice. "Oh, my God! Are you hurt?"

She couldn't speak immediately. The men knelt beside her and Jonathan's voice rose angrily, "You clumsy oaf!"

From behind them, on the path, there was the sound of a vehicle approaching very fast. Curt began to speak in a whining tone. "I lost my footing. Susan, I'm so terribly sorry. Please, forgive me. Here, can you get up? Let me help you."

Her thundering heart began to slow down and she sat up gingerly. "I'm all right—I think."

The approaching vehicle wasn't the Rolls, which they had left at the road, for it sounded too loud for Jonathan's car. The vehicle came to a skidding halt and there was a creak as a door was opened, then slammed shut. Jonathan and Curt were helping her to her feet.

"Take it easy now," Jonathan said soothingly. "Go slowly. Maybe we should carry you to the car."

"No, it isn't necessary." Susan stood on her feet, leaning against Jonathan, and took in several deep breaths.

A black man appeared on the knoll. "I saw you from the lane," he announced abruptly. "Can I help?" He was wearing worn brown twill trousers, a khaki shirt and a stained straw hat. It was a moment before Susan recognized him, for she'd only see him a few times and at some distance. It was Abraham Jaimes, Mala's husband.

"Thank you for stopping," Jonathan said to him. "The lady has had a rather nasty accident." He didn't appear to recognize Abraham and, indeed, it was probable that he'd never seen him before. Nor did Curt seem to know who he was, for he looked at the black man with a blank expression. What was one of Travis's workmen doing so far from the plantation in the middle of the day? Susan started to say his name, but then she saw that Abraham was gazing at her as if he'd never seen her before. For one confused moment, she imagined that there was a warning in Abraham's still expression, and her acknowledgment of him died in her throat.

Was it possible that he *didn't* know who she was? If not, then she might be able to keep what had just happened from Travis, after all. He would have a fit if he learned she'd fallen, and Susan could hardly blame him. It *had* been careless of her to go climbing about alone on such uneven ground. She should have waited for the men in the lane.

"I'm all right," she said, standing straight and

taking hesitant steps toward the car. "Really, I am."

Jonathan and Curt each took an arm to help her along the path. Abraham stood motionless, watching them, until they passed the jeep he had been driving and were back in the Rolls. Jonathan insisted that she lie down in the back seat, and he and Curt got into the front with the driver.

The Rolls moved forward. "Look, that jeep's right on our tail," Curt said after a few moments. From her prone position in the back seat, Susan couldn't see the road, but she knew that Curt was speaking of Abraham. Maybe he *had* recognized her and meant to follow them back to the plantation to assure himself that she was all right. Then, of course, he would go straight to Travis. She closed her eyes and tried not to think about it.

At the house, Jonathan helped her inside. Mala heard them and came into the entryway.

"Mrs. Sennett had a fall," Jonathan told her. "She should lie down."

Mala looked frightened and began to make little clucking sounds as she urged Susan toward the living room. "Better not try the stairs until the doctor sees you."

"You're both making too much fuss," Susan insisted. "I'm not hurt, except for a few scratches on my knees."

She lay on the couch and Jonathan stood beside her, anxious and frowning. "Jonathan, stop looking so worried."

Mala hovered beside Jonathan for a moment.

"I call Dr. Elliott." She ignored Susan's protests and went to the telephone that stood on a table at the end of the couch.

"You—you'd better go," Susan said in a low voice to Jonathan. "The doctor will convince them I'm all right." She didn't add that she didn't want him there when Travis came in, and she was certain that Abraham had gone to find him.

But he seemed to understand. "Yes, perhaps you're right. I—I can't tell you how responsible I feel for what happened. I should never have allowed you to leave the car. I'll phone you later to see what the doctor says." He was gone by the time Mala had finished her telephone conversation.

Whatever the black woman said got Dr. Elliott there within twenty minutes. In the meantime, Mala had cleansed Susan's scraped knees and applied a healing salve. Travis was with the doctor when he came into the living room. They must have met at the front door.

Dr. Elliott pulled a chair over next to the couch and opened his black bag, pulling out his stethoscope. As he listened for the baby's heartbeat and questioned Susan, Travis stood beside the couch, looking grim and quite angry.

Finally the doctor said, "Mother and baby seem fine. I think you should stay in bed for a couple of days, just as a precaution, Susan. Whatever you do, don't go for any more hikes."

Relieved at the prognosis, Susan murmured an agreement. "If you have any pain, call me immediately," Dr. Elliott went on. "Since you've chosen home delivery, I'd better be with you from the beginning. Sometimes a first baby can be difficult."

As Travis showed the doctor out, she left the couch and headed for the stairs, refusing Mala's offer of aid. But Travis returned in time to see her intention and, cursing at her foolhardiness, scooped her into his arms and carried her up to her room. She clung to his neck, her cheek pressed against his chest. The strong, steady beat of his heart drummed in her ear.

He laid her on the bed and unbuckled her sandals, removing them. Then he sat beside her and smoothed back from her face the long strands of hair that had escaped the pins. He looked into her eyes anxiously. "When Abraham found me and told me what had happened—" He broke off, swallowing. "I went through hell until I got back here and the doctor said you were all right."

"It was all a lot of excitement over nothing," Susan insisted.

He made a sound of impatience. "I've tried to be tolerant, but this tears it. I don't want you to see Wicksham again. You could have been hurt —lost the baby."

She sighed tiredly. "But I wasn't. There's no harm done."

"I could strangle him with my bare hands. This time I'm going to him and lay down the law."

"I'm the one who went walking where I shouldn't have. Besides, it wasn't Jonathan's idea to go out into the country. It was Curt."

"Curt!" The frown lines etched even more deeply between his brows. "He was with you?"

She nodded, wishing, too late, that she hadn't mentioned Curt. "He wanted Jonathan to look at some land. They're thinking of going into business together."

"Don't be naive, Susan! Why would Wicksham want to go into business with someone like my cousin?"

She turned on her side, away from him. "I don't know and I don't care. Just let me rest."

She could feel his anger and knew that he wanted to know more about what had happened that afternoon. But he left the room, and she moved restlessly on the bed until she found a relatively comfortable position.

She had no intention of talking to Travis again about her fall. It had happened because of her own carelessness, but fortunately she and the baby were unhurt. The way Travis had acted, anyone would think that Curt and Jonathan had wanted her to fall! She knew why he was in such an unreasonable state. If she had not been so lucky, she could have lost the baby—his heir, as he had so pointedly reminded her. That was what had frightened him so badly. She closed her eyes and forced back resentment. Soon she was asleep.

She was allowed to leave her bed two days later, with the stipulation from Dr. Elliott that she keep to the house. She had expected Jonathan to phone, as he had promised, and on her first trip downstairs she questioned Mala.

"Have there been any phone calls for me?"

Mala, who was serving her lunch, thought for a moment. "Miz Harte called yesterday. She comin' out to see you this afternoon, I think."

It was perhaps a measure of Susan's boredom that she accepted this announcement with some degree of anticipation. "Weren't there any other calls? What about Mr. Wicksham?"

Mala looked blank and shook her head. "No'm, nobody else."

Susan knew that there was only one explanation for Jonathan's failure to inquire about her. Travis had indeed gone to him, as he had threatened, and told him not to contact his wife again. The high-handedness of it made her fume. She sheer arrogance of Travis's thinking he could decide whom she might speak to on the telephone was beyond belief. But there was little she could do about it at the moment, she thought angrily, as she felt the baby kick. She *could* tell Travis again that she would pick her own friends, and she decided to do it that very evening.

She was in the sitting room reading a baby-care manual that she'd purchased months ago when Kay Harte appeared in the doorway carrying a bouquet of yellow roses in a hand-painted Italian vase.

"Mala said I should come on back." Kay announced, walking into the room.

"Hello, Kay." Susan laid the manual aside. She had it practically memorized by now, anyway. "How did you know I have a thing for yellow roses?" She accepted the vase, admiring the bouquet from several angles before setting it down on a low table. "They're beautiful. Thank you."

Kay looked crisp and cool in her pink shirtwaist dress. She took a chair and admitted,

"Travis mentioned once—oh, months ago—that you're crazy about yellow roses. I had the devil of a time finding them in Bridgetown, and then the last florist I called had them."

"You shouldn't have gone to so much trouble."

"No trouble," Kay said, smiling. "Tell me, how are you feeling after your little accident?"

Evidently Travis had told her about what had happened in the country. How many times had he talked to her since the accident, Susan wondered. Did he see her or phone her every day? With some effort, she squeezed these thoughts from her mind. "I feel about as well as anyone can, under the circumstances." She made a face. "Good heavens, you look skinny!"

Kay laughed. "You're going to have your figure back in no time. When's the little stranger due?"

Surely Travis had told her, but Susan played the game of polite conversation. "Six days from today, and I hope he's not going to be late."

"He? You've decided it's going to be a boy, have you?"

Susan had been thinking of the baby in those terms for several weeks now, she realized. She made a gesture of mock-helplessness. "Travis wants a son, and my husband always gets what he wants."

Kay's dark brows rose quizzically. "Did he say that he wants a boy?"

Susan shrugged. "He didn't have to. I think I know how his mind works by now."

Kay leaned forward in her chair, a look of hesitation on her face. Then she said, "From what Travis has told me, I'm not sure you know him as well as you think."

216

Susan's determination to deal with Kay's call with cool grace slipped a little. "Perhaps. Apparently I don't know him as well as you, since he seems to keep you so well informed."

Kay looked as if she'd been slapped. "I'm not sure what you mean by that, but Travis and I do see each other every week or so. When he's in town, he usually stops by my shop for a cup of tea. We've known each other all our lives. I'm sure it never occurred to him to break off our friendship when he married, but if it bothers you . . ."

"Why should it bother me?" Susan's tone was touched with sarcasm, in spite of her effort to pretend indifference.

"I—I don't know why." Kay was looking even more perplexed. "It shouldn't." She gave a little gasp of startlement. "You can't think there's anything going on between Travis and me!"

"Frankly, Kay, I couldn't care less." Susan had begun to twist her hands in her lap. To hide her unease, she picked up a flowered throw pillow and held it against her stomach. "Look, we might as well be frank with each other. I know you're probably the only person on Barbados who Travis told about his grandfather's will."

Kay was pensive for a moment. "Yes, and I'm sure he wished the words back the minute they were out of his mouth. He'd just found the will, you see, and he was so angry. He felt betrayed by his grandfather. It happened that I saw him shortly after he'd learned the truth. I wanted to invite him to a card party. I could tell something was wrong, and when I questioned him it all came out in a rush. If I hadn't been there at that moment, he would never have confided in me."

"Lucky for you that you were," responded Susan airily. "Otherwise, you might have been in my place."

The dark eyes were baffled. "In your place? You mean married to Travis?" The bafflement changed to a flash of pain, the same look Susan had seen in Kay's eyes when she first realized that Travis had married someone else.

"Truthfully, if he hadn't blundered and told you about the will, wouldn't you have said yes?"

Kay regarded her gravely for a long moment. Then she murmured, "I'd have married Travis under almost any conditions, if he'd ever asked me. Until that day when you first walked into my shop, I dreamed of that happening. Foolish of me, but I kept telling myself that one day Travis would look at me and suddenly see me as the right wife for him. The will wouldn't have made any difference to me at all if that had happened."

Susan stared into the other woman's clear brown eyes. "Are you saying that Travis never proposed to you?"

Kay shook her head and uttered an embarrassed laugh. "I gave him plenty of opportunities, too. I did everything but propose to *him* that day when he told me about the will. If he realized what I was doing, he didn't let on. I've been grateful for that ever since. I made rather an embarrassment of myself, actually." She took a long breath. "I don't know anything about how you and Travis met, but I've suspected lately that you were unaware of the provisions of the will until after you were married. Susan, it doesn't matter that he failed to tell you in the beginning, does it? You're his wife and you're having his child. I wonder if you realize how very fortunate you are."

The last thing Susan needed was for this woman who loved Travis to urge her to count her blessings. Had Travis put her up to it? She was relieved to see Mala approaching. "Would you like a cold drink, Kay? I've consumed gallons of iced tea these past few days. Our air conditioning has been off as often as it's been on. We're still waiting for a repairman."

"Iced tea sounds fine," Kay said. "The scarcity of good repairmen is one of our trials here. I believe Travis is involved in that new trade school they're building in Bridgetown. We desperately need more trained workers, and they're expecting the unemployed to flock to the school when it's completed—those who can afford the small tuition. The last time I talked to Travis, he said something about arranging low-interest loans through his bank for qualified students."

Kay continued to talk about the trade school and other projects under way on the island to bring down the high unemployment rate. Susan listened with interest, making little comment. She didn't want Kay to know that Travis had never mentioned any of it to her. That might have been because she had given him little opportunity. They shared little conversation these days, and when they did, it inevitably seemed to deteriorate quickly into an argument.

After Kay had gone, Susan, thinking back over the conversation, realized that she had been wrong in assuming that Kay had been Travis's first choice as a wife. She was sure that Kay had been telling the truth; she wasn't a woman who dissembled. Not that the knowledge changed anything as far as Susan and Travis were concerned. He probably hadn't wanted to ruin a perfectly satisfactory relationship by marrying Kay, Susan told herself. Yet Travis said there was not, never had been, an affair. Could she believe him? And did it really matter to her if it were true? Travis's lack of romantic interest in Kay didn't mean that he loved Susan.

That evening after dinner, Travis came into her bedroom with a coffee tray. He set it down on a side table and angled the room's two upholstered chairs on either side of it.

Susan, who had been sitting at the dressing table brushing her hair, turned to watch him silently.

"Come and sit over here," Travis said. "You didn't wait for your usual cup of coffee after dinner, so I've brought it to you." He filled two cups as Susan came across the room. She was already dressed for bed in a full white gown and matching peignoir.

"Coffee didn't sound appetizing earlier, but now that the air conditioning is back on—for the moment, anyway—I think I could drink a cup." She tried to make herself comfortable in the chair.

Travis took the other chair. "You were unusually quiet all through dinner," he remarked.

"You didn't even mention that you had a visitor today."

"Kay—yes. I suppose Mala told you? We had a nice chat."

He lifted his cup in both hands and relaxed against the padded chair back. "Good. You know that I've always hoped you and Kay could be close."

Susan looked at him over the rim of her cup. "Is that why you sent her out here? To tell me what a lucky woman I am?"

He frowned, setting the cup down. "I didn't send her. I didn't even know she was coming."

Susan sighed tiredly, not wanting to pursue the topic suddenly. It didn't matter. Nothing seemed to matter much lately. Then she remembered the decision she'd made earlier in the day. "I want to ask you something. Jonathan hasn't phoned since my accident, and there has to be a reason. Did you tell him not to?"

His jaw tightened for a moment and then he said, "Yes. I told you I'd had it with that business. If you refuse to protect yourself, somebody has to."

"Protect myself—from *Jonathan*?"

"He's a dangerous man." The words were grim.

Susan was incredulous. "That's the most ridiculous thing I've ever heard! I think you really believe it, too. You can't stand the thought of my having a friendship with another man, so you've convinced yourself he's up to something underhanded." She glared at him. "I won't let you do this! I'm going to see Jonathan whenever and wherever I choose, and there is nothing you can do or say to stop me!"

He was scowling darkly. "You're getting upset. We'll discuss this later."

"No! There's nothing to discuss. I've made my position clear enough—*Oh!*" Suddenly her hand shook and she set her cup aside.

He came to alertness, sitting on the edge of his chair. "What's wrong?"

A second pain stabbed at her and she gasped. "I'm not sure—but I think it's the baby."

He was on his feet instantly, helping her to stand. "You must lie down." He steered her to the bed where she lay, looking up at him with wide eyes, and tried to remain calm. "I've had a dull ache in my back all day, but just now it moved around to my stomach." She swallowed the dryness in her throat. "There's no reason for concern. It'll probably be hours yet—if it isn't a false alarm—but maybe you ought to call Dr. Elliott."

His hands shook visibly as he thrust them into his trouser pockets. He surveyed her with deep concern. He was in worse shape than she was! "I'll send Mala up to stay with you. Then I'll phone Dr. Elliott and that nurse who's on stand-by." Still, he didn't move. "Are you sure it's all right to leave you—just until Mala comes?"

She started to laugh, but the sound ended in a gasp as another pain gripped her. "I'm not going anywhere, believe me. Now go on. Nobody has a first baby in less than two or three hours."

He left her reluctantly, muttering that he should have had telephones installed in all the bedrooms months ago. Susan began to breathe in short, shallow pants as the doctor had shown her. It was supposed to ease the pain and delay the baby's birth until the doctor arrived. But the pains were severe already, and she prayed that Travis could reach Dr. Elliott right away.

Chapter Twelve

*H*er body was one vast landscape of pain. At first there had been valleys of quiet exhaustion between the rending upheavals, but now there was only a huge agony that came in waves, one only beginning to recede when the next began. Perspiration bathed her and occasionally a cool cloth was pressed against her cheeks and forehead, and at those times she saw Mala's distressed face swimming above her. Sometimes she knew that Travis sat beside the bed and held her hand, and when the pain crested she gripped with all her might.

A sharp medicinal smell mingled with the faint aroma of tobacco. Once in her twisting and turning the blackness of the window impressed itself upon her awareness, and she realized that it was very late at night. She had no conception of how long she had struggled in this morass of pain, for she had begun to drift into periods of unconsciousness, though whether these periods were momentary or long she didn't know.

And sometimes there were voices.

"I should never have agreed to her having this baby at home. I'll never forgive myself if . . ."

"We're doing everything that could be done in a hospital." This voice was calmer. "Why don't you have a drink, go for a walk."

"No."

"The baby's large and in the breech position. I'm going to try to turn it. Go into the hall and leave her to the nurse and me for a few minutes."

"No."

"For God's sake, stand back then. I haven't time to deal with two patients."

The pain was wrenching her apart, and she felt herself falling into an abyss where there was escape and surcease. Later, she drifted back to consciousness and heard the same two voices, the one tired-sounding but reassuring, like a rippling stream, the other ragged and agitated.

"It's head first now, and nature will take its course very soon. Susan, can you hear me? Don't fight the pains, push with them."

"She can't take any more of this!" the ragged voice said, the tone driven, as if the speaker were also in pain. "Can't you give her something?"

"That would only delay things. It'll be over in a few minutes now."

Over . . . over . . . over. The word echoed in her head, and on another crescendo of pain, she heard the ragged voice again. "If it comes to a choice, you are to save Susan. Is that understood? I want my wife!"

"Yes, yes." The calm voice sounded only half attentive. "Mala, make him sit down over there. Get him a drink. That's good, Susan. You're doing fine."

* * *

She was surrounded by light, warm and golden. She opened her heavy-lidded eyes. She lay in her bed in a yellow gown, although she had been wearing a white one the evening before. Shafts of sunlight bisected the room and fell across the foot of the bed. She felt the tangled mass of her hair and groaned softly. Where was her brush?

"You've decided to join us, have you?" A tall, white-uniformed woman with serene blue eyes stood beside the bed, smiling.

Susan tried to shake the remnants of sleep from her brain. "Are you the nurse?"

"That's right, Mrs. Sennett. I'm Dot Howard and we've already been through a lot together, you and I."

"I—I don't remember very much."

"Honey, that's nature's way of making sure women will keep on having babies. We never remember the pain of birth afterward."

"Was I in labor a long time?"

"Six hours. It must have seemed like ages to you, though. Your labor was rougher than some because the baby was in the breech position until the very end. That prolonged things, but I've been on hand for even longer deliveries. It was your husband's first, poor man, and we had our hands full with you and trying to keep him out of the way, too."

"The baby—is it all right?"

The nurse chuckled. "That one's right as rain. He's got Mala dancing attendance on him already. Bawls his head off when he doesn't get what he wants the second he wants it."

He. She had a son. "I want to see him."

"Of course you do. He's in the nursery. I'll go get him."

"Before you go, would you please hand me my hair brush?" Susan sat up, feeling a lovely lightness. She ran her hand over the flatness of her stomach and smiled at Dot Howard. "I have to look my best when I meet my son."

The nurse handed her the brush. "I've brought a basin of water and a cloth, too. You can shower this afternoon, but for now let's make do with the basin."

While the nurse was gone, Susan lathered rose-scented soap on the soft wash cloth and scrubbed her face and hands. Then she brushed the tangles from her hair and arranged the pillows comfortably at her back. She felt like a new woman.

Dot entered the room carrying a white bundle. She laid it in Susan's arms. The baby was wrapped loosely in a thin, cotton covering with only his head showing. His eyes were closed, but he was moving and making little fretting sounds. His head was well shaped and capped by a shock of black hair. Susan looked into the face of her son and felt a welling of emotion that was unlike anything she had ever felt before. She blinked away the moisture in her eyes and folded back the covering to examine the little, warm body dressed only in a diaper and undershirt.

"Well, he's got ten fingers and ten toes," she said to the nurse, surprised at the unsteadiness of her voice. She held him close and kissed the downy softness of his cheek. "Oh, isn't he wonderful?"

Dot laughed. "You don't think I'm crazy enough to disagree with a new mother about that, do you?"

The baby's fist found its way to his mouth and he began to suck loudly. "My little man is hungry," Susan cooed. "Will I have milk yet?"

The nurse helped her slip down the strap of her gown. "Let this bruiser at you, and you'll have milk before the day's over."

The baby found her breast and began to nurse contentedly. "Goodness, he's strong," Susan said, "for such a tiny person."

"You haven't seen many newborns apparently. He weighs nine pounds and is twenty-two inches long. That's a big baby."

When the baby had finished nursing, Susan let the nurse take him reluctantly. "I want you to rest until after noon," Dot said. "Don't worry. He'll be squalling for more in two or three hours." Dot carried the baby away and Susan laid her head back on the pillows with a sigh.

A moment later, Travis came into the room. He looked haggard. Unshaved stubble darkened his face and exhaustion dulled his eyes.

"You look awful," Susan greeted him, still feeling the lingering joy that holding the baby had given her. "Who had this baby, anyway?"

He sat down on the bed beside her, reaching for both her hands, which he squeezed so tightly that she winced. "Have you seen him yet?"

"The nurse just took him back to the nursery. He—he's so beautiful."

His mouth twisted wryly. "I don't know about

beautiful. He was red and screaming his head off when I tried to hold him. Mala said I was scaring him, but I'm the one who was scared. I kept thinking how small and helpless he looked." A flash of pain crossed his face. "Oh, God, Susan, I thought he was going to kill you."

If it comes to a choice, you are to save Susan. I want my wife. From some forgotten corner of her brain, the words surfaced. Had she really heard him say them at some point during the long night? Or had her imagination conjured up the words, mixing them with the confusion of dreams and pain?

She stirred self-consciously under his gaze. "Dot Howard seems to think it was a pretty normal birth. She said she'd assisted at longer deliveries than this one."

He shook his head once, an expression of disbelief in his eyes. "If that was normal, I hope never to see an abnormal one."

"I thought I heard the doctor telling you to leave the room. Why didn't you?"

"I couldn't leave you alone while you were in such pain, and yet there was nothing I could do to help. I've never felt so useless in my life."

The earnestness of his voice touched her, but she didn't want to be touched by him. She was too weak just yet to deal with that. "I guess we should give him a name. Would you like to call him Travis?" She hadn't known she was going to suggest that until the words were out.

He gazed into her eyes for a moment without speaking. Then, "I have another idea. Why don't we give him your maiden name?"

"Warren Sennett." Susan listened to the sound

of it. She suspected that all men liked the idea of a son bearing their name, regardless of what Travis said. They could give him both names. "Warren Travis Sennett. That sounds nice and substantial. I like it."

"I'll tell the doctor then—for the birth certificate." His eyes held hers, and she thought he was going to say something more. But he got to his feet. "I'm going to shower and shave and catch a nap."

She wrinkled her nose. "I'm dying to get into the shower. Dot says I can get up this afternoon."

"Don't try to rush anything," he said a little anxiously. "Okay?"

She nodded, wondering if he was referring to more than her getting up.

"Good. I'll see you in a while."

He left her, and she lay, staring up at the ceiling. Had she really heard that anguished plea to save her, even at the cost of the baby's life? She couldn't believe it. Without the baby, Travis would lose his inheritance. No, she must have imagined it. Suddenly her arms ached to hold her child again and she drew a long, unsteady breath. There was now no doubt about one thing: She could never go away and leave the baby behind. She wasn't capable of it. So, what was she to do?

She closed her eyes. Later, she told herself. She would decide later when she had her strength back.

After lunch, the nurse brought the baby to her again, and when he was returned to the nursery,

Susan was finally allowed to get up. While she showered and washed her hair, Mala changed the linens on her bed, thrusting her head into the bathroom every few moments to check on Susan.

In a fresh gown, her hair wrapped in a towel, Susan came back into the bedroom. Mala was running a dust cloth over the furniture. "I was about to come and see if you were all right," the older woman said.

Susan sat down in a chair and began to towel dry her hair. "You're worse than Travis, do you know that? I've only had a baby, for heaven's sake. Millions of women do it every day."

Mala's white teeth flashed in a grin. "Maybe I worry so 'cause you been unhappy lately. Things be all right now."

Surprised at Mala's perceptiveness, Susan murmured something noncommital and began to brush her hair. She wished that she could feel as certain as Mala did that things would work out.

"That phone ringing off the hook all mornin'," Mala told her. "Everybody hear about the baby and want to know how much he weigh, what's his name."

Susan smiled. Any scrap of news traveled throughout the island almost as soon as it occurred. Gossip seemed to be a favorite Barbados pastime.

After Mala left, Travis came in carrying four floral arrangements in his arms; he set them in various spots around the room. He'd shaved and changed clothes, and he looked more rested than he had earlier. "The yellow and white roses are from me," he told her.

"Thank you," she murmured.

"The carnations are from the Williams. You remember, we had dinner with them a couple of months ago? Kay sent the ivy—and the orchids are from Wicksham." He grinned at her wryly, then added with reluctance, "He's a better loser than I thought."

"Loser?" Susan asked. "What has he lost?"

"You—your company, for one thing. He'll never try to contact you again. I made sure of that."

A familiar feeling of resentment stirred in Susan. "Why do you refuse to let me have friends?"

He sank into a chair and ran both hands through his hair, disordering its brushed smoothness. "That isn't true. I *want* you to have friends."

"Then why are you being so stubborn and impossible in this case?"

"Because I know Wicksham better than you do."

Susan laid her brush aside and leaned back in her chair. Her sigh was pure exasperation. "You've hinted before that there's something sinister about Jonathan. But, Travis, unless you can give me some good reason, I'll continue to count Jonathan as a friend and behave accordingly."

He studied her thoughtfully. "I didn't want to upset you before the baby came. You were always so tired and tense. But it seems I have to tell you now or you're going to keep rushing headlong into things that you've no idea of. Do you remember what I told you once about a small group of men who are trying to take over the government of the island?"

She nodded, silenced by his serious tone.

"I've suspected for a long time that Jonathan Wicksham is the moving force behind all our problems in that area. He has the money to finance a coup."

"A coup!" Susan was staring at him. "Are you suggesting that Jonathan is a—a revolutionary?"

He shrugged. "It happens to be to his advantage to avoid bloodshed and work through the opposition political party. I can't prove all my suspicions yet, but the evidence against him is growing all the time. We know now that he's hired men to mix with the unemployed and stir them up against the government and certain people that Wicksham sees as threats to his control of the island. I'm one of those people, Susan. I suspected from the beginning that he befriended you simply because you are my wife. He even tried to win you over with that rhetoric about the old families owning too much land at the expense of the poor."

"If you know this, why isn't somebody doing something about it?"

"We are, and we'll do more when there's enough evidence to keep him out of the country for good."

Susan felt bewildered, and she shook her head. "It's obvious that you believe what you're saying, but I can't. Jonathan has never been anything but kind to me."

"Even when he almost caused you to lose the baby?"

This was even more of a shock than what had gone before, and denial crowded into her throat. "That's preposterous! It was an accident."

"Was it?"

Her gaze faltered and she looked away from him, frowning. "Even if it wasn't, it was Curt who lost his footing and fell against me."

"I see," he stated ominously. "I should have known Wicksham wouldn't do his own dirty work. Curt left Barbados early this morning, by the way, as soon as he heard about the baby."

None of this was making sense to Susan. Jonathan had called Curt a clumsy oaf, and she had thought it was because he had caused her to fall. Could it be, instead, that it was because he hadn't caused her more serious harm? "What has the baby got to do with anything?"

He rubbed the back of his neck, trying to sound calm and reasonable in the face of her disinclination to accept what he was saying. "Wicksham wants me out of Barbados because he knows I'm on to him, and he also knows that the only circumstance under which I'd leave would be if there was nothing to hold me here. Curt wants me to lose control of the plantation and bank, too, but for quite different reasons. Apparently they decided to work together to achieve a mutually beneficial end." He lifted his head to look gravely into her eyes. "If you had lost the baby, I'd have had no heir and Curt and Violet would have come into two-thirds of my holdings here. They would have forced a sale and I would have had no reason to stay."

Was it possible that Curt and Jonathan *had* been conspiring together?"

"I think," Travis went on, "that Violet learned what they were up to and, to her credit, wanted no part of it. Which is why she left here alone so abruptly. That piece of land Curt claimed to be considering for tourist cabins isn't for sale. I checked."

"Are you saying that Curt and Jonathan took me out there for the purpose of staging an accident?" She swallowed the sudden fright that dried her mouth.

He nodded. "I'd been expecting them to pull something before the baby was born, but it never occurred to me that they would try to hurt you. I didn't realize they had become so desperate. I'd have stopped Wicksham's seeing you months ago if I had." His words had become jerky, each one painful to utter. "Fortunately, I'd taken the precaution of having one of my men follow you whenever you went anywhere with Wicksham."

Abraham! So that's how he had happened to be in that desolate location in the middle of a work day. If Travis was right, Abraham might very well have saved her life—and the baby's.

She thought of Jonathan's kind gray eyes, his unfailingly solicitous manner toward her. But she also remembered that he had brought the word "abortion" into their conversation and had assured her that he could find a doctor who would do it. Now that she thought about it, it did seem rather farfetched for a successful business entrepreneur like Jonathan to consider forming a partnership with someone as weak and irresponsible as Curt Winston. It made a sick kind of sense that the "small enterprise" Jonathan had mentioned was a plan to ensure that Travis had no heir. The thought made her tremble with delayed reaction and she looked at Travis with stricken eyes.

"Why didn't you tell me all this long ago?"

"Would you have believed me? Lately you've been determined to pursue whatever course I opposed. Besides, I never guessed that Wicksham's opposition would take such a personal turn. I thought he'd befriended you merely to get information from you concerning my activities. I expected him to try to discredit me in the political realm."

It was true that she probably wouldn't have believed him. After all, he had warned her that Jonathan was dangerous and she had reacted with scorn. She thought of her son, the miracle of that precious bundle of life that she had so recently held in her arms for the first time. A wave of pure hatred and maternal protectiveness rose in her, making her feel sick. If she ever saw Jonathan again, she would want to fly into his face like a mother cat protecting her young with unsheathed claws.

"I never suspected," she murmured. She shuddered suddenly. "I think I could cheerfully kill him."

Travis's expression was portentous. "Now you know what I've been going through, watching you spend more and more time with him and unable to make you see that you should stop. I've given Wicksham one week to leave Barbados for an extended vacation or face being charged with assault against you. Abraham will testify against him. We might not be able to get a conviction, but Wicksham doesn't want the publicity of a trial and his name spread all over the newspapers."

"I—I'm glad you finally told me everything."

He smiled ruefully. "That may be the first thing we've agreed on in months." He unfolded his long length from the chair, standing with an abrupt movement. "I'll let you rest now. We have to have a long talk, though, when you're fully recovered."

She watched him go and, for a brief moment, she saw him as the man she had met in Miami, the man she had fallen in love with, the man she had thought to be everything she ever dreamed of in a husband.

A wave of infinite sadness overwhelmed her. How, in so short a time, could everything have gone so wrong?

Chapter Thirteen

*B*ank business took Travis to New York a few days later and, from there, contacts he wanted to make as a representative of his political party took him to Washington. He was gone for more than three weeks, checking in with Susan by phone every day or two. These long distance conversations dealt mostly with the baby and his progress. Travis apparently felt, as she did, that they couldn't discuss their personal lives satisfactorily with so many miles between them.

Susan used the time to good advantage. A daily routine for the baby was established, but with Mala and Dot on hand to help with him she still had a good deal of time to herself. Much of it she spent walking on the beach, thinking and renewing her strength. She was sitting in one of her favorite spots near the plantation's private cove on a promontory overlooking the sea when she decided it was time to give serious thought to her future and that of her son. She had come almost every day to this spot to watch the lashing waves batter themselves on the jagged reef that ran out from the land for several hundred yards. The unending roar of the surf was in tune with the stormy confusion that thundered in her brain.

Today, as she gazed out at the foaming crests, she felt a stilling of her inner turmoil, and the new serenity brought tears that overflowed and trickled silently down her cheeks. She sat there for more than an hour, long after the tears had stopped, her thoughts following the alternatives open to her, one by one, to their logical conclusions. When she rose, she felt depleted, but composed. Not fully recovered emotionally . . . it would take a little more time for that to be accomplished, but ready to set out on the only course that would lead to that recovery.

The birth of her son, the days since then and her tears had raised a wall between herself and her resentment. For the first time since she had learned about Harris Sennett's will, she was truly strong enough to face whatever had to be . . . and knew it.

She walked back to the old Sennett mansion with a straight back and a lifted chin. Now she knew what she was capable of doing—and what she could not do. She had plans to make and a fresh start to prepare for. At last she could face Travis calmly and talk everything out with total candor.

In the days that remained until Travis returned, she went about her activities with a readier smile and a lighter step than before. For long, quiet times she held her son in her arms as he nursed and slept, and she never tired of wondering at the beauty and perfection of this child that was a part of her and of Travis. There was no longer any feeling of pressure or urgency.

Decisions would have to be made when Travis returned, but until then the days were for renewal and building inner strength.

She also began to make use of the kitchen as if she had a right to do so and not as a guest. She and Mala worked side by side for hours, planning and cooking meals, and chatting as friends. And each afternoon she prepared an elaborate tea tray which she shared with Dot Howard in the nursery as her son slept nearby.

In her eyes there was a mature serenity that had not been there before. She had known passion and love and heartache and betrayal, and now she knew that her life would go on and that she would find fulfillment and satisfaction again, perhaps not soon, perhaps not easily—but with her son to give a focus to her life, it could be good once more.

On the last evening before Travis's expected return, she took a thermos of coffee down to the cove. She sat on a sea-scarred rock, as battered as she had felt not long ago. She poured coffee into the thermos's plastic screw-on cap and cradled its warmth between her hands. She leaned back against a water-smoothed section of the rock and felt the wind-carried salt spray on her face.

The pale sliver of a quarter-moon glimmered far out over the water near the horizon. The ceaseless swoosh of the waves created an almost chantlike background to her thoughts as she sipped from her cup and felt her body relax.

Inexorable. Travis had used that word to describe the sea, and for the first time since coming to the island she felt a part of the inexorability of all things. Life was inexorable; in spite of individual pain and disillusionment, it went on, and the pain dulled, and eventually went away when the sufferer learned to let it go. When at last she left the rock and walked back to the house, she felt purged and free.

Travis pulled his car into the garage, got out wearily and lifted his suitcases from the trunk. In the house the lights were on in several of the second floor rooms and in the ground floor study. His plane had been delayed and the dinner hour was long past; he had eaten a meal that tasted like cardboard on the last leg of the flight. The lines fanning out from his eyes were more than squint marks; tonight they were deep slashes of worry and strain. He had welcomed the hectic pace of the past three weeks and the business that had kept him away from home. The time had provided a respite before the inevitable confrontation. But now there was no more possibility of delay, and his face was the face of a man who knows that everything that matters to his future will be decided before the sunrise. He no longer fought against the knowledge.

He gripped his suitcases and walked slowly toward the house. He had had many sleepless night hours during the past weeks to wonder if he had ultimately destroyed Susan's ability to trust and love him, or any man, again. What price had he made her pay for his arrogant decision to take all that she had to give, while deceiving her?

He had hoped to force her to love him again by keeping her with him until the baby was born, but now he was dreadfully afraid that he had succeeded only in driving her so far away that he could never hope to reach her. What if she still wanted the divorce? What if . . .

He shook his head as he stepped onto the back veranda, trying to clear his mind of the guilt that had burrowed into the secret crevices of his brain to mock him at every turn. His body ached with more than tiredness. It ached for her as strongly as it had ever ached during these last, lonely months. Sometimes at night he still dreamed that he was holding her and awoke to the empty spaces—in his arms and in his heart —as he called her name.

He had kept her with him physically, but in every other way she had shut herself off from him. It was slowly killing him, and he had only himself to blame. As selfish and greedy as Harris Sennett had ever dreamed of being, he, Harris's grandson, had grabbed what he wanted with no thought for the consequences to her or to himself.

He set one of the suitcases down and placed his hand on the door knob. He opened the door, retrieved the suitcase and walked into the back hall, which was dark and still. Leaving the luggage there, he moved down the hall, finding his way without the aid of lights from years of familiarity with the house. Instinctively he went toward the study, where the door stood open and light spilled out into the hall. He stopped in the doorway, staring, unable to speak, afraid to speak for fear that what he saw was merely what he wanted to see.

Susan sat at his desk, bent over one of the

plantation ledgers, a pen in her hand. She wore a pale blue silk robe with wide sleeves, and her hair, unrestrained by combs or pins, fell forward, half covering her face like a silver-white veil in the lamplight.

Travis's starving senses drank in the sight of her slender figure, the graceful lines of her half-hidden profile, the creamy ivory skin. There was a calmness and maturity in the concentrated expression that had not been there three weeks ago.

Then, perhaps sensing that she was being watched, she looked up at him, coolly and directly.

"Hello, Travis."

He watched her soft lips form the words and heard the low syllables.

"Susan." It was all he could say immediately. He felt as uncertain as an adolescent experiencing puppy love for the first time, and his voice stuck in his throat. There was so much that he wanted to say and, in spite of all his carefully prepared speeches, he suddenly had no idea where to start. For a moment, it was enough just to look at her.

Susan saw the haunted look in his eyes, the lines of strain in his face, and knew that these past months had not been easy for him, either. She had been too centered in self-pity to see it clearly before.

"You're working." The statement sounded foolish; Travis's voice stumbled on the words as if he were unused to speaking at all.

"The baby will sleep for a couple of hours yet, and I wanted something to do." She spoke casually, composedly. "You've arrived much later than we expected. You must be tired."

"Yes," he replied, coming farther into the room, then hesitating.

She closed the ledger and folded her arms on the desk in front of her. "We have some decisions to make." She said it so quietly that it took a moment for her meaning to strike him and when it did, he lowered himself into a leather armchair, knowing that his reprieve was at an end. Then he met her steady, emerald eyes and braced himself.

Susan saw his expression change from apprehension to hardening resolve, and she felt a slight tightening of all her muscles. Did he still think he could force her to live by his rules? Hadn't he yet learned that there was a world of difference between a life freely chosen and the same life pursued under duress?

"You look well," he said, forcing a semblance of detachment into his tone. She looked so feminine and beautiful that it made his throat ache with immense pain. He longed to touch her, to kiss her, to lose himself in her soft, sweet flesh.

"I've been caring for the baby and the house and going for long walks," she informed him. "And I've been thinking a great deal."

"So have I," he muttered, only half aloud. He looked at her and came abruptly to his feet and began to pace back and forth. "Oh, God, Susan, I've missed you!" He stopped pacing and faced her, legs spread, jaw hard.

He might have come around the desk, but the implacable green fire in her eyes stopped him. "I have some questions to ask you, Travis."

He thrust his hands into his trouser pockets and waited.

"When you came to my dressing room that first time in Miami, had you already made up your mind to marry me?" Her words were hard.

"No!" He rubbed the back of his neck, then looked around a little helplessly. He gestured toward the couch. "I—I think this may take some time. Can we sit on the couch?" He smiled slightly, but his eyes were sad. "I promise not to touch you if you don't want me to."

After a moment's hesitation, she nodded, then followed him to the couch, where she curled up in a corner. Travis sat down at the other end and ran his hands through his hair. Susan watched him silently as he lighted a cheroot.

He drew on the cheroot, then said, "I came into the Top Hat the first night merely for a meal and a drink. Then you came on stage and sang and I was intrigued by you. No, more than intrigued. I thought you were the most beautiful woman I'd ever seen, and I wanted to know you. I came back the second night just to see you again. When I asked you to have dinner with me, I wasn't thinking about the will or marriage or anything except that I wanted to spend some time with you alone."

The words were rough and hesitant at first, and then they came faster, surer, as he continued talking. "After that, I couldn't stay away from you. I found you more sexually exciting than any woman I'd ever known, and when I began to suspect that you might feel something of the same thing for me, I wanted you so badly I could taste it."

He leaned forward, took another drag on the cheroot, put his elbows on his knees and stared at the floor between his feet.

"It was all I could do to walk away from you the first time I kissed you, but I was afraid of coming on too fast. I didn't want to rush you or make you think I was only interested in getting you into bed."

She responded quietly, with a wry smile. "I was glad that you walked away—but I wanted you, too."

He looked up, meeting her rueful gaze. "I know. I sensed your mixed feelings, and that's why I backed off. I meant to give you more time to get to know me, but the next night, when I held you in my arms, all my good intentions went right out the window."

He got up, walked to the desk and stubbed out the cheroot in an ashtray. He returned to the couch. "During the night, while you were sleeping, I lay awake and tried to make some sense out of what was happening between us. I knew it was too fast, but I decided to ask you to marry me. I wanted to tell you about the will then, but I was sure you would think that was the reason I proposed. I thought that if I could get you to marry me, bring you back here, give you a chance to get to know me better, I could prove myself to you before you found out about the will." He laughed gratingly. "Instead, you learned about it at the worst possible time, and in the worst possible way—and drew the worst possible conclusion."

"I want to know exactly how you felt about me on our wedding day, Travis."

He sat back on the couch and looked directly at her. "I'm trying to be as honest as I know how to be. Looking back, I think the realization of how deep my feelings for you went came to me gradually. If the will hadn't been a fact, I would have given you more time to get used to the idea before I asked you to marry me—and myself time to sort out my feelings. But knowing what I did about my inheritance, I panicked. I lost whatever self-confidence I might have had and steam-rolled you into marrying me immediately. I know now that I felt more than sexual attraction for you from the beginning. If I hadn't been in such a panic, I would have known it then. By the time we stood before the judge, I was already deeply in love with you, Susan—you have to believe that."

She was still, thoughtful, staring at her hands, which lay quietly in her lap. "I think perhaps I can believe that now because of something that happened—at least, I think it happened—while I was in labor." She looked up and pushed back her hair with one hand. "I thought I heard you tell Dr. Elliott that if it came to a choice between my life and the baby's, you wanted him to save me. Did you really say that?"

"Yes, and I meant every word of it! I stood in that room and watched you suffer, hour after hour, and all because of me, and everything that I thought I wanted was suddenly of no importance. I realized how unfair to you I'd been since the day we met and I knew that, without you, all the land and money in the world would mean nothing." His expression was so agonized that she didn't doubt him for a moment.

"I remembered your words the next day," she said, "but I wouldn't believe right away that I had really heard them. It was the same as when you told me that Kay wasn't your mistress. At some level, I knew you were telling the truth, but I wouldn't accept it. When Kay told me that she would have married you at any time if you had asked, I realized that you had chosen to marry *me* instead of Kay or any other woman, but I still felt used. I suppose I wanted to nurse my disillusionment and resentment a little longer."

There was a tired twist to his mouth. "I can understand that. You said that you've done a lot of thinking while I've been gone. Well, so have I, and last night I finally decided I had to give you whatever you want. You can leave Barbados if that's your choice. I'll agree to a divorce."

She spoke softly. "What about the baby?"

"You can have custody for at least half the time. If you choose to go, you can take Warren with you." The words were ragged, each one a piece of himself torn out forcibly against his will. He seemed to brace himself to receive a killing wound. "Just tell me what you want, Susan."

"I've had my own dark night of the soul while you were gone," she told him huskily, "and I've made a decision, too." She looked at him, and her love was naked and unabashed in her eyes. "I want to stay here. I want to be a wife to you and a mother to Warren. I want us to be a family. I want to forget the hurt we've inflicted on each other. I love you, my darling—and I want to make you love me so desperately that you'll never regret this marriage for a single moment."

An inarticulate sound escaped Travis, a sound of tremendous release and triumphant joy. His arms came out, reaching for her, pushing her down on the couch beneath him.

A shuddering sigh ran through both of them, though where it started and where it ended they could not have said. With reverent, trembling hands, he began to trace the outlines of her face, as if he were a blind man who had to assure himself that the one he loved was really with him. His fingers caressed the line of her jaw and throat, moving down to part the soft fabric of her robe and linger on her swollen breasts, stroking and delighting in their weight and silky smoothness.

"My love—my wife," he whispered with such unsteadiness that sympathetic tears rose in Susan's throat.

She closed her eyes, savoring the wonders of his touch, a touch that she had denied herself for so long. She had been empty and starved without him, and she knew now that she needed his touch, his nearness, his love, to be complete.

Savored pleasure quickly turned to leaping fire, and she gave herself to her husband, holding nothing back, just as he opened the deepest recesses of himself to her, offering her all that he was and had. They murmured all the words that lovers everywhere say to each other in such rapturous moments, but on their lips the words seemed infused with special meanings understood by themselves alone.

They made love with an intensity that touched

every cell and nerve, every hidden aspect of their beings. They achieved a oneness that was magical and mysterious and unspeakably wonderful.

Much later, they turned out the lights and climbed the stairs, arms about each other, to begin their true marriage and to build a dynasty.

If you enjoyed this book...

...you will enjoy a Special Edition Book Club membership even more.

It will bring you each new title, as soon as it is published every month, delivered right to your door.

15-Day Free Trial Offer

We will send you 6 new Silhouette Special Editions to keep for 15 days absolutely free! If you decide not to keep them, send them back to us, you pay nothing. But if you enjoy them as much as we think you will, keep them and pay the invoice enclosed with your trial shipment. You will then automatically become a member of the Special Edition Book Club and receive 6 more romances every month. There is no minimum number of books to buy and you can cancel at any time.

Coming Next Month

Tears Of Yesterday by Mary Lynn Baxter

Paige and Lane Morgan had once shared the secret joys of marriage, but they had been unable to make the magic last. Given a second chance, they must find their way into each other's arms through a glittering, jewelled maze to reach a place where time and sorrow have no meaning, where a touch, a whisper, a silent stare are all.

A Time To Love by Billie Douglass

From the land of hurt and fear, Arielle Pasteur came to beautiful St. Maarten seeking only to be alone. But Chris Howe had no intention of allowing her to hide. Something in this beautiful, alluringly innocent woman called to him, and with his loving touch he smoothed life into her body and erased the scars of the past with his promises for the future.

Heather's Song by Diana Palmer

Cole Everett watched Heather Shaw grow from a child into a girl hovering on the edge of womanhood. She had a body ripe for love, a heart ripe for a man's invasion. She sang songs of love, a love she didn't fully understand, but with Cole's help she would leave innocence behind and taste the fruits of knowledge and desire.

Silhouette Special Edition

Coming Next Month

Mixed Blessing by Tracy Sinclair

In Europe, home of elegant traditions and
enduring romance, Holly and Slade lived out a
love story of their own. He demanded to hold her
close, to sear her with his touch and be seared in
return. She desired to teach him the lessons of
loving and giving. Together they kindled a
passion that flamed across a continent and
turned an ocean to fire.

Stormy Challenge by Stephanie James

Leya Brandon thought her heart was protected
against Court Tremayne, but she had
underestimated his determination to win her for
his own. He set out on a campaign to challenge
her heart and storm the barriers of her mind.
And before he finished, he would leave her
hungering for his lean strength, shivering
at his gaze, and aching for the fulfillment
only he could give.

Foxfire Light by Janet Dailey

In the wooded Ozark hills, Linc's gold-flecked
eyes mocked her. His country-born spirit clashed
with her city-wise ways. His lean body sparked
her senses till Joanna was glowing as sweetly
as the foxfire that lit their nights. This
wasn't an impetuous dream, but a
bright and shining love to light
the way to tomorrow.

MORE ROMANCE FOR
A SPECIAL WAY TO RELAX

$1.95 each

1 ☐ TERMS OF SURRENDER
Dailey

2 ☐ INTIMATE STRANGERS
Hastings

3 ☐ MEXICAN RHAPSODY
Dixon

4 ☐ VALAQUEZ BRIDE
Vitek

5 ☐ PARADISE POSTPONED
Converse

6 ☐ SEARCH FOR A NEW DAWN
Douglass

7 ☐ SILVER MIST
Stanford

8 ☐ KEYS TO DANIEL'S HOUSE
Halston

9 ☐ ALL OUR TOMORROWS
Baxter

10 ☐ TEXAS ROSE
Thiels

11 ☐ LOVE IS SURRENDER
Thornton

12 ☐ NEVER GIVE YOUR HEART
Sinclair

13 ☐ BITTER VICTORY
Beckman

14 ☐ EYE OF THE HURRICANE
Keene

15 ☐ DANGEROUS MAGIC
James

16 ☐ MAYAN MOON
Carr

17 ☐ SO MANY TOMORROWS
John

18 ☐ A WOMAN'S PLACE
Hamilton

19 ☐ DECEMBER'S WINE
Shaw

20 ☐ NORTHERN LIGHTS
Musgrave

21 ☐ ROUGH DIAMOND
Hastings

22 ☐ ALL THAT GLITTERS
Howard

23 ☐ LOVE'S GOLDEN SHADOW
Charles

24 ☐ GAMBLE OF DESIRE
Dixon

25 ☐ TEARS AND RED ROSES
Hardy

26 ☐ A FLIGHT OF SWALLOWS
Scott

27 ☐ A MAN WITH DOUBTS
Wisdom

28 ☐ THE FLAMING TREE
Ripy

29 ☐ YEARNING OF ANGELS
Bergen

30 ☐ BRIDE IN BARBADOS
Stephens

Silhouette Desire 15-Day Trial Offer

A new romance series that explores contemporary relationships in exciting detail

Four Silhouette Desire romances, free for 15 days!
We'll send you four new Silhouette Desire romances to look over for 15 days, absolutely free! If you decide not to keep the books, return them and owe nothing.

Four books a month, free home delivery. If you like Silhouette Desire romances as much as we think you will, keep them and return your payment with the invoice. Then we will send you four new books every month to preview, just as soon as they are published. You pay only for the books you decide to keep, and you never pay postage and handling.

READERS' COMMENTS ON SILHOUETTE SPECIAL EDITIONS:

"I just finished reading the first six Silhouette Special Edition Books and I had to take the opportunity to write you and tell you how much I enjoyed them. I enjoyed all the authors in this series. Best wishes on your Silhouette Special Editions line and many thanks."

—B.H.*, Jackson, OH

"The Special Editions are really special and I enjoyed them very much! I am looking forward to next month's books."

—R.M.W.*, Melbourne, FL

"I've just finished reading four of your first six Special Editions and I enjoyed them very much. I like the more sensual detail and longer stories. I will look forward each month to your new Special Editions."

—L.S.*, Visalia, CA

"Silhouette Special Editions are — 1.) Superb! 2.) Great! 3.) Delicious! 4.) Fantastic! . . . Did I leave anything out? These are books that an adult woman can read . . . I love them!"

—H.C.*, Monterey Park, CA

* names available on request